The TAMING of Lilah May

BAD gal

Vanessa Curtis

F

FRANCES LINCOLN
CHILDREN'S BOOKS

First published in Great Britain in 2011 and the USA in 2012 by
Frances Lincoln Children's Books, 4 Torriano Mews,
Torriano Avenue, London NW5 2RZ
www.franceslincoln.com

A catalogue record for this book is available from the British Library.

ISBN 978-1-84780-149-4

Set in Palatino

Printed in Croydon, Surrey, UK by CPI Bookmarque Ltd. in March 2011

1 3 5 7 9 8 6 4 2

For Susan, in memory of Sarah.

CHAPTER ONE

Uh-oh.

I've done it now.

And I don't even really care.

I step over Amelie Warner where she's lying stunned on the floor and I sit back down at my desk, heart pounding and hands clenched.

Miss Gorman is bearing down on me like a swirling tornado of wrath, all flapping grey cardigan and flopping pearl necklace. I catch a whiff of the revolting perfume that she insists on wearing and I begin to feel like a bowl of instant whip being whisked up into a stiff peak, except that instead of being pink and sweet, I'm angry and red as if somebody's bled into the bowl.

'May!' she says. 'Get to the front of the class. NOW.'

I get up and drag my feet towards the blackboard and make vile faces while my back is turned to the rest of the class.

'Copy the first page of this book onto the blackboard,' she says. 'And make it quick.'

She hands me a Natural History book and I start writing up some rubbish about frogs and ponds with a piece of chalk that makes the hair on my arms stand to attention every time I scratch it across the board. I can't be bothered, so I just chalk up the words 'I can't be bothered', over and over, until the class starts sniggering and she turns around.

Next, I write the word '*Groo*'. No, even that word isn't strong enough for me today.

I woke up in the blackest, foulest mood you can imagine.

The wind was howling up and down our street and the sky looked as if somebody had switched the lights off for good.

My mother forced me to eat lumpy porridge while she applied her weird make-up at the kitchen table, and my father left for work with a dart gun over his shoulder. I was left staring at the picture of that boy on our fridge, and asking myself for about the zillionth time, *Why?*

And as usual, there was a silence only filled by the hum of the fridge, and the kitchen threatened to swallow me up with my own thoughts, so in the end I slung my bag over my shoulder and headed here to school to try and drown out my anger.

And now the Gorman has stormed up to the blackboard and is hanging over me like a grey boulder rocking out of balance on the edge of a craggy cliff – one more push from me and she'll tumble down, crushing all life out of my weary body.

Go on, says the angry voice in my head. *Just do it.*

I drop the chalk on the floor and slowly grind it to a white, powdery mess under my black school shoes.

There's an audible gasp from the more sensitive members of the class.

Out of the corner of my eye I see my best mate, Bindi, bury her dark head in her arms and shake it slowly from side to side.

Miss Gorman gets a dustpan and brush and sweeps up the chalk with short, abrupt gestures.

Then she grabs me by the shoulders, propels me out of the door, down the corridor with its lines of lockers and smell of old cabbage, and onto the bench outside the headmistress's office.

'I don't know what's got into you, May,' she says. The anger has gone out of her now, and she's kind of sunk into a pile of grey clothes next to me. Her warm shoulder presses up against mine. I don't move, even though I kind of want to.

'I mean – we know about your situation at home. But surely you must be ready to try and get on with your life by now? Was there really any need to push another pupil off their chair?'

An image of Amelie Warner lying stunned on the floor, her eyes wide with fear, flashes through my head and I feel the first wave of horrid guilt wash over me.

'She was teasing me about my parents,' I say. 'She said that it's no wonder I've turned out to be a freak.'

Miss Gorman sighs and shakes her head.

'Oh, Lilah,' she says. 'Striking out is not the answer. You do know that, don't you?'

For a moment I catch her eye and she looks concerned, like a real person and not just a teacher. I feel bad for about a nano-second. It's not her fault that I'm angry. She carries on with her firm gaze and it's tempting to tell her everything.

But I'm too tired. How can I explain that I'm sick

of my parents being obsessed with their jobs, and that there is a huge great vacuum in our house that just won't fill up?

The light outside the headmistress's office changes from red to green.

That's my cue to go inside.

I get up and let Miss Gorman open the door for me.

'Lilah May, Miss Hendricks,' she says with a weary smile. 'Again.'

Then she pushes me inside and disappears.

I hear her heels clicking back down the shiny corridor and the faint bang of the classroom door.

Then I sit down in the black leather chair to await my fate.

CHAPTER TWO

<u>LILAH'S ANGER DIARY</u>   MARCH 6th
ANGER LEVELS : <u>9/10</u>

I got another detention. The headmistress told me that if I get one more, I'll be expelled. I felt kind of excited when she said that 'cos I hate school. Then I felt guilty thinking about Mum and Dad, and how they save and budget so that they can afford to send me there.

Then the guilt and the excitement just got drowned in another big wave of red rage, so I skived off the last lesson of the day and sat on the swings in the park, kicking at the gravel until the black leather on the toe of my shoe was all streaked with white dust.

Adam Carter, the hottest boy in the entire world,

was sitting on the swings when I got there. He was bunking off Chemistry, so we got talking, and now I've agreed to meet up with him later on. Mum will go mental if I tell her about it so I'm going to have to rope Bindi in to do some covering up for me.

Bindi texted me to find out where I was. She came and sat on the swing next to me and asked me what my anger feels like. But I couldn't explain it while she was looking at me with her big, serious eyes, so I've saved it to write in my diary instead.

This is what my anger feels like:

Kicking a door really hard when I've forgotten to put my trainers on.

Someone's nails digging into my palm until my eyes water and the blood rushes around my ears.

A screw stuck into my chest and being tightened with a screwdriver.

A barbecue set alight in my stomach, and little spits and hisses of heat shooting up around my soft guts.

Burning hot rain falling from a dark red sky.

I've been angry for two years.

I'm angry most of the time.

No.

Not most.

Make that all.

* * *

So I'm home from school, and I'm trapped in the kitchen like a ball of fire that wants to spread through the house but can't.

I want to get ready to see Adam Carter, but Mum's gearing up to ask me That Question.

I can tell it's coming, because she has just turned around from the sink and given me an intense, scowling sort of frown.

The frown doesn't match her outfit.

She's wearing black and white baggy checked trousers, a matching long-sleeved top with a huge white frilly ruff around the neck, giant red shiny lace-up shoes and a small, black bowler hat.

In case you think my mother is some kind of demented nutcase with no fashion sense, I ought to point out that actually she's a clown.

No, really, she is. She runs a business that organises clowns for children's parties.

There's something dead weird about watching somebody in a clown's outfit doing the washing-up just like a normal mother.

Dad's not much better. He's wearing boring

clothes but it's a certain bet that his mind is only full of one thing. Lions.

My dad's a lion tamer.

Yeah. That tends to kill quite a lot of conversations stone dead, at least for a moment or so. Most people think that lion tamers are some Victorian thing, involving circus big tops and crowds of women in long stripy dresses fainting as the brave lion man does some sort of freak show, perhaps accompanied by a dwarf or two, and a man with a big handlebar moustache.

Well, maybe it was like that in the Olden Days.

But now 'lion tamer' is just a name for somebody who looks after the lions and tigers in a zoo, which is what my father does. To give him his full title, he's Head of Big Cats at Morley Zoo.

He's a solid bloke, my dad, all hair shaved to a number one and hard muscles. He's got a tattoo of a green mermaid with long red hair all the way down one arm and my mum's name, Rachel, written in black inside a red heart on the other. I reckon the big cats know when they're beaten.

Don't ask me how he went from serving as a chef in Her Majesty's Army to confronting lions, leopards and cheetahs on a daily basis, but somehow his career path took an unexpected turn and chucked him towards the jaws of the big cats.

He's standing in the kitchen doorway with his shirtsleeves rolled up and his hands on his hips. His body language screams *I-don't-know-what-to-do-with-my-mental-teenage-daughter*.

'*Groo*,' I say. That's a Lilah-ism. I've invented loads of these words for when I can't find real ones that explain what I'm feeling inside. I've got a whole list of Lilah-isms for various different occasions. I can select them just like I choose an outfit every day.

'Make it quick,' I say. 'I'm going out again soon.'

Both of them are now looking at me as if I am a breed apart. Or an alien daughter, beamed down from Planet Zarg to replace the apple-cheeked violin-playing prodigy they'd have liked to bring home from the hospital fifteen years ago. Hah! That's kind of rich, them looking at ME like I'm the weird one!

My cheeks are pale as goat's cheese and I don't play the violin. My sort of music needs to be played loud and is the source of much arguing between The Old Dudes and me.

I live on Planet Rock. It's a radio station.

It's also my spiritual home.

My mother dries her hands on a scrunched-up tea towel with a picture of Windsor Castle on it, and sits down at the kitchen table. She pulls out a small mirror and starts to remove the big white circles around her eyes.

'I had twenty of the little buggers earlier,' she says. 'I suppose I shouldn't complain, but sometimes I wonder why their parents can't just take them to McDonalds and have done with it, and then I could stay home and watch *Emmerdale* instead.'

I know.

Sad.

It's not surprising I've turned out so twisted.

Mum and Dad are now doing that thing parents do, where they start raising their eyebrows at one another and looking towards their troublesome offspring.

'Erm, Lilah,' begins Mum. She stops for a moment to pull a false eyelash off, and then has to fish it out of her wine glass and run to the sink to rinse it clean.

Oh, the 'Lilah' thing. Yes, that's my strange name. It's short for Delilah, but obviously I can't go around using that. Not unless I want to spend my final few years at school as a total social outcast. My parents have this obsessive love of names from the Bible, which is a bit weird, as neither of them are exactly church-going types. My brother's called Jacob but he was quick to shorten it to Jay, which, if you ask me, probably saved his reputation at school too and even made him sound quite cool.

Jay May.

Not that there's much point asking me any questions about Jay.

I get up from the kitchen table, where I've been hacking my name into the wood with a pencil.

'Gotta go, programme's starting,' I mutter. Then I make for a quick exit, but Dad's all fired up today. His reaction times are impressive. One minute he's sitting at the table, the next he's blocking the doorway. I almost forgot that he works with large, dangerous animals for a living and is ex-Army to boot, all darting eyes and big rippling muscles.

'Not so fast, hotshot,' he says. I have no idea where these nicknames come from. But they're, like, *so* yesterday. *Hotshot?*

I slump down back at the table. Defeated – for now. I'll get my revenge with the new Slipknot album later on.

'The thing is, Lilah,' says Mum, 'we want to ask you something. We don't want you to get offended. We're just trying to help.'

Oh no. My soul starts to slide towards my black Uggs like thawing clumps of snow.

I wish they wouldn't start trying to HELP me. I mean – that's what I've got a best friend for, isn't it? Parents are just there to make dinner and tell you off.

'Yeah?' I say. 'What?'

Mum reaches out and holds my hand. Hers is slimy with greasepaint and make-up. Yuk. Now I'm itching to get away.

'Lilah,' she says. 'How ARE you? You seem so angry all the time. It's been two years.'

I feel the prickles of anger starting up in my gut again.

I really, really hate it when people ask me this question. *How ARE you?* It's mainly adults who come out with it. They always have this kind of soppy look on their faces when they ask it, and they say it in a sort of hushed, low voice that reminds me of something on an American chat show.

It's the worst question in the world, because I just can't answer it in any way that is honest, and it makes my eyes sting and my heart thump and my teeth clamp together and my arms fold tight across my chest.

'Fine,' I say. That's what I always say. It's a complete lie, of course, but I can't tell Mum how I'm really feeling inside without the risk of shouting at her that of course I'm not fine, I'm probably never going to be fine again and I've never felt less fine in my whole life. So I just stick to that one word and I try to keep all my churning feelings of rage inside.

A silence greets my answer. It fills our heads with moving pictures from old home videos. Seeing them is torture. It's like a knife twisting deep in my guts.

I know that we're all seeing different pictures. Mine are full of childhood and light and sand and laughter. I don't know what Mum is seeing, but I'm guessing that it's babies and nursery and school uniform with nametags sewn inside. Dad has turned away so that I can't see what he is thinking, but it's probably football matches and homework and trips to the zoo.

I can feel the prickles of anger starting up in my gut again.

My eyes fill up with hot water.

The tears never fall down my cheeks. It's like they've got to stop just short of my bottom eyelids or else I'll go to pieces.

I haven't done proper crying for over two years.

I scrape my chair back and leave the room.

***

I pass Jay's bedroom door as I go upstairs.

Closed, as usual.

I aim a swift kick at the wood with the toe of my boot and then curse when it hurts.

I go into my bedroom and take a good look at myself in the mirror.

I want to see whether all the crap I'm feeling on the inside is visible on the outside, but I still look like the same old Lilah May. Glossy shoulder-length black hair, sallow complexion the colour of onion skin, glaring dark blue eyes, and a defiant look in them, too.

I sink onto the bed with a sigh.

My parents are right. Not that I'd give them the satisfaction of telling them so.

I'm still angry.

Too angry.

I just about keep it under wraps when I'm with Bindi, but something about being at home makes me into this seething ball of wrath.

I pick up my mobile and dial Bindi. Even the thought of tapping in a text message makes me feel cross, and I hate predictive texting, so I just dial her number and wait until her slightly breathless voice answers. Bindi always sounds as if she's expecting some major adventure to happen. She's kind of the opposite of me – hopeful, wide-eyed, like she can't wait to grow up and live her life and make her mark on the big world.

Innocent. That's the word I'd use for Bindi. But then, she seems to have the perfect home life, and I don't.

I'd stay in bed every day if I could, with a duvet pulled right over my head to block out any chink of light.

'Yes, who is it, hello?' says Bindi's voice.

She hasn't worked out that you can save numbers on your phone so that you can see who's calling you. I've given up trying to make Bindi move into the twenty-first century.

'It's me,' I say. 'Lilah. You know – your best mate. That Lilah.'

Bindi gives her little chuckle.

'You crack me up, Lilah May,' she says.

'Yeah, I'm hilarious,' I say. But I'm smiling again.

That's what's good about Bindi. She really likes me just for being me, even though she knows everything about me.

Everything.

And not all of it is good.

There's no way that my parents are ever going to agree to me going out with Adam Carter tonight, so I have to rope Bindi into a devious plan.

Bindi does not like deception. She's the most honest person I've ever met. I just can't imagine Bindi ever lying. Ever.

'Why can't you just tell your parents the truth?' she says. There's the sound of screaming in the background and the harassed voice of Bindi's mum, Reeta, trying to separate two of the youngest members of the family. 'They like Adam, don't they?'

I sigh.

`Yeah,' I say. `They like him because he's a friend, but if I said I was meeting him on my own they'd lose their cool.'

I squirm on the bed where I'm sitting in a pair of black jeans with my legs crossed and my hair falling like silk around my face in its post–school liberation.

'I'm going to have to say I'm with you,' I tell Bindi.

'But then your mum will ring my mum, and my mum's not going to lie for you, Lilah. I can tell you that now.'

I roll my eyes – she can't see me anyway – and flop back onto the bed, sticking my legs up into the air and observing my blue and white stripy socks.

'Well, then – you're going to have to pretend to be your mum and answer the phone,' I say.

I know I'm putting Bindi on the spot here, but nothing can be allowed to ruin my wonderful evening with Adam Carter. He is only like the most gorgeous boy in the entire school. He's sixteen and plays in a band called Death of Love. They're thrash metal and really good.

The trouble is, Adam might be all tough when he's in the band, but when he's not, he likes girls to be all feminine and pretty and small and laughing. Which is just about the opposite of me. I'm a tomboy, attractive rather than pretty, taller than most girls in my class, and I definitely have not done much laughing of late. That's why I was surprised when he suggested meeting up.

After lots of pleading and begging and persuasion, not to mention a bit of bribery (I've promised to buy Bindi any lunch she wants for the next week), Bindi agrees to help.

'Thanks,' I say. 'You're a true best mate.'

There's another loud scream from an indignant child in the background.

I laugh.

'Is that Adi?' I ask. Adi is the youngest in Bindi's household. 'He's so sweet.'

It's Bindi's turn to give a big sigh now.

'Not always so sweet,' she replies. 'He'll do anything to get attention. Some of us don't get a look in.'

'Oh,' I say, but I don't really believe her. Bindi's parents are very proud of her.

'OK, I'll cover for you later,' Bindi is saying. 'You're a nightmare, Lilah May.'

I smile and hang up the phone.

She like *so* loves me.

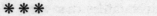

19

Mum never has time to cook during the week.

She's standing in the kitchen gulping from a new glass of red wine and dishing up a shepherd's pie that she made at the weekend and then shoved in the freezer.

There are tiny baby carrots to go with it, and a dish of leafy kale.

Dad's gone out on an emergency lion-call so it's just the two of us.

That's nothing new. It's hardly ever the three of us these days.

'Mum,' I start, stirring my fork around in the savoury mince so that a strong smell of animal and onion rises up towards my fringe. 'Is it OK if I go round to Bindi's in about an hour? She wants to play me some CD or something.'

Mum looks up from where she's forking in mince in a vague sort of a way. I know she's thinking about Jay.

'I'll give her mum a call, just to make sure,' she says, going over to the phone.

I cross my fingers hard underneath the table. I've arranged with Bindi that she will hog the phone all evening.

'Reeta?' Mum's saying. 'How are you?'

There's a short pause. I'm hoping that it's Bindi she's speaking to, not Reeta.

'Lovely,' Mum says. 'Actually Reeta, Lilah would like to come over and see Bindi for a while. I hope that's OK with you?'

Whoever's on the phone obviously says that it is, because Mum says, 'Thanks, love,' and hangs up with a smile.

'Yes, that's fine,' she says to me.

Megatriff!

'Poor Reeta,' says Mum. 'She sounds as if she's got a terrible cold.'

I fight back a smile.

Bindi's such a great best mate.

'You don't need to call there to check I've arrived,' I say, rinsing my plate in the sink and gulping down a glass of water. 'I'll only be a couple of hours, tops. Promise.'

'OK,' says Mum. She looks a little nervous. There weren't all these rules and curfews and checking-ups when Jay was my age.

'Thanks for supper,' I say, bolting upstairs.

I stand in front of my mirror and decide to stay in the black jeans, but change into a tight black and white striped top and some silver hoop earrings.

I spray gloss stuff all over my dark hair and put my eyeliner on again for about the millionth time today. Then I lace up a pair of black Converse trainers and fling my black leather jacket over the top.

'See you later,' I call to Mum, rushing out of the front door before she can see how much make-up I've got on.

I leap onto my bike and wheel off towards the precinct, wobbling in the stiff breeze.

There's something strange in the air tonight.

Or maybe it's just me.

It's like everything is sharpened and extra-clear after the storm earlier.

I swear I can even smell a hint of danger in the air.

It makes me feel reckless and mad and confident.

I chain up my bike and stroll into the precinct.

Adam's there early, which is kind of good as I have absolutely zero patience and hate waiting around for people.

He's got his back to me, so I creep up by the fountain where he's standing, and then some mad urge makes me leap on his back and shout

'ADAM!' so that both of us almost fall into the water.

'You nearly gave me a heart attack, Liles,' he says, brushing down his black T-shirt and tossing back his hair.

Liles?

When has he ever called me that?

That's the special name that Jay had for me.

'Call me Lilah,' I say, abruptly.

He stares at me for a moment, but then his good-natured grin returns and he offers me a hand to jump off the side of the fountain.

'Where shall we go?' he says.

I shrug.

'Park?' I say. It's a mellow sort of evening now, still and full of promise.

'Sure,' says Adam. He pulls a roll-up from his pocket and sticks it between his lips.

'Smoke?' he says, offering me the packet of dried worm tobacco.

'No thanks,' I say. 'Smoking is for idiots.'

He gives me a surprised look at that.

I can see why. I mean, I look like a girl who'd smoke. I'm wearing a rock-chick outfit, after all, and I've got the attitude to go with it.

But there are things that Adam doesn't understand.

Things from the days of Jay and me.

'I thought you'd—' he starts.

'I said no,' I repeat, firmer.

There's a very packed silence, full of questions and apologies and disappointment.

Oh, mushcats, I think. *This date hasn't got off to a very good start.*

'I like your jacket,' I say, trying to make my voice softer.

'Thanks,' he says. 'Got it off eBay for three quid.'

I give him a new look of respect. He's obviously got an eye for a bargain. And he does look dead gorgeous.

'So how ARE you?' he's saying now. Uh-oh. He asks this while staring straight ahead. Most people can't look me in the eye when they come up with the question. It's awkward for them.

It's even more awkward for me. He's asked my worst ever question.

I take a long, deep breath through my gritted teeth and kick one of my feet against the other. It's only a little movement, but it makes me feel a bit better.

'Yeah, OK,' I say, all casual. 'Nothing's changed much.'

Adam flashes me a look of sympathy and then clears his throat.

'So,' he says. 'Do you still want to go to the park?'

I shrug.

I haven't really given the evening much thought. All my energies have been focused on getting to the fountain in the precinct and looking gorgeous for Adam. But I guess we'll have to do something – we can't hang around the closed shops all evening.

'OK,' I say. 'Park's fine.'

We set off down the road. I'm ultra-aware of how close Adam's body is to mine as we walk along the pavement. I hold myself very straight and try not to brush against him, but sometimes it just happens, and a little shock of excitement pulsates up from my legs to my stomach.

Thanks, Bindi, I think. I've got some serious making-up to do next week.

We've reached the high iron gates of the local park.

Adam pushes one of them open and holds it

for me while I duck under his arm and head towards the swings.

'You're a bit old for that, aren't you?' he says, as I plonk myself onto an orange plastic swing and watch my black-jeaned legs fly up in the air and over his head.

'So?' I say.

He's pointing to the sign now. It says, *No children over fourteen.*

'It's OK, I look young for my age,' I shout from where I'm flying backwards with my hair streaming out behind me and the silver hoops pulling in my ears.

I don't tell him that I used to play on these swings with Jay when we were little.

Some things are too painful and private to ever say, even with a Lilah-ism.

Adam sits down next to me and does some slow swinging back and forth, but I can tell that he's not that impressed so I swing down again, bit by bit, and then skid to a stop with my trainers in the gravel.

We walk the length of the park, chatting about this and that, but all the time I'm wondering if he's bored and if I've made a big mistake thinking that he liked me, because he's acting quite casual and distant.

And although he smiles at me, it's not a smile with much warmth behind it, but more a careful, measured smile kept for friends who just happen to be girls.

After we've done the park we wander into a local cemetery.

I like gravestones. Don't know why. There's just something solid and comforting about them. The last home of the dead. Kind of like the end of an exhausting journey. It's like a big, quiet, safe club full of people who can't shout at me to tidy my room or brush my hair. In fact, it's the only big gathering of adults I feel comfortable with.

I perch on top of a tomb shaped like a treasure chest, and Adam sits on the grass at my feet and rolls up another cigarette. After a pause, which is loaded with meaning and anticipation and stuff, and just when I'm sure he's about to say something really amazing to me, he looks up from beneath his wing of fair hair and says, 'You know something? You kind of scare me, Lilah May.'

Then he gives an abrupt laugh and becomes very busy with stuffing the tobacco worms into his cigarette paper again.

Somewhere behind the wall of the cemetery, the sun finally starts to sink down, leaving a blank grey sky and an edge to the air.

I zip up my leather jacket and hug my elbows.

I scare him?

'But you're the one in the big hard rock band,' I say. 'You're far more scary than I am.'

Adam smiles at this, but still looks a bit wary.

Great.

This date is going about as wrong as it could do. Or, to be more exact, it isn't exactly going anywhere at all.

So I'm frightening. I scare people.

I never used to scare Jay. It was more the other way round, particularly towards the end.

I get up, and toss my hair back over my shoulders.

'Maybe I should do something scary, then,' I say. 'Kind of live up to your expectations, huh?'

Adam gets to his feet and lights his cigarette.

'Don't be stupid,' he says. 'We're good mates, yeah? You can just be yourself, can't you?'

My heart flops to the grass beneath his feet and is trampled to death underneath his red Converse boots.

Mates.

I feel like an idiot now. It's all Bindi and her

stupid suggestions. She kept passing me messages in class saying he was staring at me. How can she have got it so wrong? He doesn't like me at all in that way.

I feel the little flicker again. Red-hot, rising up from my feet towards my chest.

I can't see my own face, but I know what it looks like.

Tight. Pinched. Lips sucked in. Eyes dark and cold.

Anger sucks all my prettiness out of me.

I head off towards the cemetery wall.

I don't yet know what I'm going to do, but my feet seem to be carrying me wherever they want and I've got no control over them.

'Lilah,' calls Adam. 'Come back. What are you doing?'

I don't answer.

I've had enough of him now.

The wall to the cemetery is high, and made of dark red bricks.

I climb onto the top of a gravestone and then launch myself at the top of the wall with my hands outstretched.

I heave myself up until I'm sitting on the top, drumming my heels against the bricks.

'Lilah,' pants Adam. He's rushed over and is staring up at me with concern. 'Don't be stupid. Get down.'

I ignore him. It feels good sitting so high up above him, with the wind in my hair.

Up here I feel all-powerful, like the world belongs to me and I'm above everything and everyone.

It's a strong wind, but I can't stop what happens next.

My legs push me up into a standing position, until I'm balancing on the thin line of bricks in my skinny jeans and my flimsy trainers.

'Oh my God,' I hear Adam say. 'Lilah. You're crazy. Please will you sit down again? I'll come up and get you.'

I laugh at that. Bit late for him to go all romantic now.

I don't care about him any more.

I don't really care about anyone.

I put my arms out, as if I'm flying, and then I balance my way, one foot in front of the other, until I've walked the whole length of the high brick wall.

Adam's face is ash-grey below me. He keeps looking around wildly to see if anybody's coming to help, but it's a cemetery on a weekday evening and there's nobody around.

I reach the far end of the wall, sit down, and then jump onto the grass far below with a thud.

Adam's there in a flash.

'Are you OK?' he asks.

I can't stop laughing.

'Your face!' I say. 'Get real! I was only walking along a wall.'

Adam's smile of relief fades to a glower.

'You stupid idiot,' he says. 'If you'd fallen, you could have broken your back, yeah?'

I lie on my stomach and laugh into the grass. Bits of it go in my mouth, but I don't much care.

Adam hauls me up and we leave the cemetery and head for home.

He refuses to speak another word until we get to the gate outside my house.

Then he glares down at me through his floppy fringe, and says:

'You're not the only person who's got issues, you know. Get over yourself, Lilah May.'

CHAPTER THREE

I go round to Bindi's house the next day to tell her about my date with Adam.

Bindi's house is like this Temple of Delights. It's about as different from my house as you can imagine.

She lives with her very large Asian family in a chaotic modern house on the other side of town from us. She's got five little sisters and one little brother and two insane, chattering and multi-tasking parents who are forever throwing their arms up in the air and shrugging their shoulders as they talk me into the ground.

I love going over to Bindi's house.

Her mum, Reeta, is an amazing cook and the house always smells of onions and savoury meat and hot, heavy, exotic spices. The kitchen is about a hundred degrees at any time of the year and there's always some sort of family crisis going on, but it's all warm and close and loving, just like a family should be.

Except that mine isn't.

Not any longer.

***

I'm up in Bindi's bedroom and we're supposed to be doing homework.

Asian Network Radio is blaring out and Bindi's weaving a long shiny ribbon into my hair, and she's put one of those red dot things right in the centre of my forehead to make me into some sort of demented goddess or something. I don't really know what she's doing, and nobody else would ever survive trying to make me look girly, but Bindi gets away with it because she's my best friend, and the thought of upsetting her would be a bit like the thought of hitting a soft, big-eyed puppy very hard.

So I don't. I sit as still as I can while she finishes my transformation into an Asian princess, and then I try on a few of her saris and spin around in front of the mirror to make her laugh.

Actually, I look quite good. My colouring's dark anyway and the dark red lipstick she's forced me to wear suits my skin tone. I've got heavy black eyeliner around my bottom lashes – I always wear that, even at school. The teachers have given up trying to expel me for it, and now they just raise their eyebrows and shake their heads whenever I pound down the school corridors, all attitude and black make-up.

'Aha,' Bindi is saying, with a satisfied smile. 'There. You can come and live with us now.'

I give her a rueful grin. 'I wish,' I say.

In fact, I'd probably be driven mental by having to live with about fifteen people in one house. But I love the fact that Bindi's family are so open and kind and that when I visit, they just sort of weave me into the fabric of the household, like I'm a missing thread that's turned up in the sewing basket.

As if to illustrate my thoughts, two of her little sisters come into the bedroom and dive onto my lap, where they fiddle with my hair and bracelets.

I like pretending that they're my sisters.

Siblings are a bit thin on the ground in our house at the moment.

My smile must have faded, because Bindi shoos her sisters out of the room.

'I'd quite like to live here with you, actually,' I say. I guess I'm hoping she'll say, 'Oh, OK then,' and I'll just be given a camp bed to put on the floor here and never have to go home again.

Bindi frowns.

'It's not always quite the paradise you're imagining,' she says. 'My parents are really strict. I'm going to have an arranged marriage, and that will have to come ahead of any career when I leave school.'

'Really?' I say. 'Wow. That sucks.'

'My parents are going to choose a boy in India and get me to marry him,' says Bindi. She sounds very matter-of-fact when she says this, like she's discussing choosing a coat in the shopping arcade or something.

'Yeah, I know what an arranged marriage is, Bindi. Just never thought you'd have to have one.'

'It's no big deal,' she says. But her mouth has drooped a bit at the corners. 'It's what a lot of Asian families do. Well, those who are still religious. Like mine.'

I shake my head. For a moment I can't speak. I try to imagine how I would feel if Mum and Dad stopped being obsessed with clowns and lions and instead focused all their energies into marrying me off to some boy I'd never met.

Groo.

'I so would hate that,' I say.

Bindi is staring down at her lap now and fiddling with the end of her dark plait.

'Well, I don't get much say in the matter,' she says. 'Sometimes it's difficult to be heard around here. Too many kids in the house.'

'Yeah,' I agree, but I'm not really listening. My head is still spinning with Bindi's revelation about the arranged marriage.

Bindi comes out of her trance and turns up the music on Asian Network.

'Now, Lilah May,' she says, settling cross-legged on the bed next to me. 'Let's hear about you. Spill.'

Bindi's the only person I can talk to about how I'm feeling.

And she's the only person I don't get angry with.

She doesn't ask me that stupid, 'How ARE you?'

question, and she's always got time for me.

Mum's too busy with her clown job and comes home exhausted and with no energy left to speak to me after yelling at groups of kids.

Dad's kind of good to talk to about some things – like how hideous my teachers are, what boring subjects I'm doing at school and what we're going to do at the weekend.

But I can't talk about the important stuff to him. You know – boys, feelings, girl stuff. He's more interested in animals than he is in me. To Dad, animals have more feelings than humans do. He's always worrying about them and reading great long articles about animal behaviour. He writes articles too, for a science magazine that deals with animals.

So I can't really talk to Dad about how I'm feeling. Teenage girls don't register on his animal radar.

The only other person I used to be able to talk to about personal stuff isn't here any more. And he got just as fed up with Mum and Dad never being around as I did.

I've got my anger diary to write in but it's not the same as talking to a Real Live Person with a sympathetic look in their eyes.

So there's just Bindi left. She's like the dustbin for all my raging tempers.

Poor Bindi.

She's staring at me now with an expectant look in her wet brown eyes.

I clear my throat and cross my legs on the bed, fiddle with my socks.

'Y'know,' I mutter. 'It's still difficult at home and all that.'

Bindi nods. She does know. She's seen me in great stomping rages after yet another argument with my parents. She's seen me quiet and withdrawn at school, and she's seen me burst into flames of rebellion and act like a complete nutter.

Bindi's always calm and serene, like the surface of a blue-green river under sunlight. She ripples with sympathy but never goes over the top.

Sometimes I wonder whether there might be a tiny flame of rebellion living deep inside Bindi. I haven't seen it yet.

'How did it go with Adam?' she says now, getting up to draw the curtains. She is smirking at me, twirling her dark plait around her finger and then sucking on the end of it. Honestly. She's so girly, she's giving off invisible pink fumes.

'It sucked – I made a right idiot of myself. Maybe YOU should go out with him,' I say.

'Don't be so stupid,' she says. She gets up and changes the CD to some other weird Asian music. 'I told you – my parents would go mad. I'm not allowed to date a non-Asian boy. Anyway, I don't fancy Adam Carter. But you do.'

My face must have fallen again, because Bindi's smile has faded too and she's looking at me with genuine concern.

'Is there still no news?' she says in a softer voice.

I shake my head. For a moment I can't speak.

Two years.

Two years.

People keep telling us that things get easier with time, but when you've got this big puzzle and you can't find the answer to it, all that happens is that the frustration and anger get bigger and bigger, until they threaten to swallow up all the nice things in your life.

'Sorry,' whispers Bindi. 'I wish I could help.'

I let my hair fall over my face.

'You do,' I say. 'You're my best mate. That helps. But don't leave me, right?'

Bindi reaches over and brushes the hair out

of my eyes with her delicate long fingers.

'Right,' she says.

We don't do a lot more talking after that.

I listen to Asian Network with Bindi and she tells me about her favourite DJ, and we test each other on Biology because we've got a mock exam tomorrow. And then Dad rings my mobile and asks if I want a lift, because he's just on his way home after dropping off the Big Cat Vet and he'll be passing near Bindi's house in a moment. I tell him not to bother, because I need the fresh air.

Then I hug Bindi and all her sisters and brother goodbye, hoist my black rucksack over my shoulders and set off on the twenty-minute walk home, except that Dad ends up driving past me anyway, so he hoots and I jump out of my skin. I climb into the van and sit there in silence while Dad talks about Hero, his biggest lion cub, who's just had some injection for something or another, and after a while I tune out his words and just stare at the windscreen wipers going back and forth. Another face pops into my head with a wide grin and curly hair, but I can't quite see his eyes any more and that panics me, so I shake the thoughts out of my head and try to focus on what Dad's telling me.

It's no good, though.

Seeing Bindi always makes me feel a bit better, but by the time I get home, that's all faded like a memory of one of those holidays which is too good to be true.

Now I am back in our white kitchen with the Aga and the big pine table and it all looks as it always does, but then there's the silence coming from upstairs, the silence that threatens to eat all of us up.

When will it ever get any easier?

CHAPTER FOUR

I haven't always been angry.

There was a time when I was smiley and happy, right up until just before I turned thirteen. Or so the photographs tell me.

The photos are too painful to look at now, so I don't. I can't see how that little girl with red cheeks and fuzzy brown hair lying on the top of a canal boat has turned into the whey-faced, black-eyed, scowling girl I see in the mirror now.

It all changed when I got to thirteen.

It's like a steel curtain whammed down and divided off the first few years of my life from the rest that lay ahead.

None of us saw it coming.

* * *

It's a week later and Dad's making supper tonight because Mum's out entertaining thirty seven-year-olds in a village hall somewhere.

Dad's hours at the zoo are a bit more regular. He's usually around in the morning to make breakfast and then again when I get home from school, unless an animal has a medical emergency. Then he leaps into his white van with the zebra-striped Morley Zoo logo and roars off to help.

I sling my bag onto the floor and slide into a chair, picking my nails and glowering at nothing.

'Fish OK?' says Dad, unwrapping a slimy paper packet all red with blood and guts. He's a health nut. Everything he cooks is drowned in great handfuls of sesame seeds and swamped with large green leafy vegetables.

'Yeah,' I say. 'But can you cut the head off mine? *Gobsome!*'

Dad hacks the head off a mackerel, wraps it back in the paper and lobs it at the bin. Something about the action reminds me of the way he throws great chunks of dead deer into the lion pen at Morley Zoo.

'Can you do the veg, Lilah?' says Dad. 'Or are they *gobsome* too?'

I get up and fill a pan, chop broccoli into little pieces and peel long orangey strips off carrots. There's not a lot of point arguing with Dad. He's built like a tank and doesn't often show a sense of humour.

Mind you, none of us do any more.

Not since that day.

We eat our dinner in silence.

It's not a bad sort of silence, like when Mum's home. She shows her feelings more, so we're always aware that we have to be careful what we say. Sometimes her eyes fill up with tears and she leaves the table and washes up with her back to us. At other times she tries too hard to be jolly and kind and smiley, and it's so awkward and embarrassing that Dad and I clam up, and then she gets angry and bitter and accuses us of never talking about the things that matter.

When it's just Dad and me, the silence is calmer. He flicks through a copy of a nature magazine while forking broccoli and carrots into his mouth.

I pick the bones out of my fish and try not to

44

think about Adam Carter. His band is playing a gig tomorrow night and I half want to go and half don't. There's this part of me that wants to get lost in the music, and head-bang and leap about shaking my hair around, and blot out all the angry and confusing stuff going on in my head. But then I know that afterwards I come crashing back down to earth, and the fallout is even worse than before.

'Ice-cream?' says Dad. He spoons pink and brown curls into my bowl and plucks himself a bunch of cloudy purple grapes from the fruit-bowl.

Then he heads off upstairs, leaving instructions for me to finish my homework and do the washing-up. I hear the click of his PC going on and guess that he's doing research on something lion-related.

I sit at the table in the quiet for a good long while. I pull out my French homework, look at it, then stuff it back in my bag again.

Part of me is actually hoping that Mum will come home. At least she'll chat away and make the effort, even if half of what she says is painful or embarrassing.

But Mum's going straight from entertaining kids to her weekly yoga class. She says it's her only way of de-stressing, after what's happened to our family.

The other part of me quite likes sitting here in the early-evening gloom with just the whine of the fridge for company.

I think about Bindi and her perfect life. She'll probably be up in her pink bedroom doing homework at the desk by her bed, her long hair falling down her back in a glossy plait and her dark eyebrows scowling with concentration. Bindi's parents will be bickering downstairs in a good-natured sort of way and her little sisters and brother will be tucked up in bed.

It's very quiet here now.

My eye wanders around the kitchen.

We don't keep many pictures of him around the house.

It's too painful.

But there's still that one on the fridge, bent with age and only held up by a tiny red fridge magnet, nearly obscured by one of Mum's endless shopping lists.

It's my favourite picture.

He's grinning towards the camera because I took it.

He's just had his ear pierced and you can see if you look closely that the lobe is still red-raw. He's got a tattoo of a black guitar on his left shoulder, and is wearing a black vest and black jeans. His hair flops forwards over one eye, like it always did. He looks crazy and loving and wired up, like he always did.

Jay. Jacob. J.

My brother. Nearly sixteen when I last saw him. Almost eighteen now.

He went missing two years, three days and nine hours ago.

Nobody's heard a thing from him since.

CHAPTER FIVE

Everyone reckons that I must have this big hole in my life since Jay went missing.

Wrong.

It's not hole-shaped, but more like something that has crept into our house and made it look different. The rooms seem the same as ever when I first go into them, except that when I'm standing in the middle of the floor and being very quiet, and the traffic has stopped and the radiator isn't humming, I realise that something isn't quite right.

It's nothing that I can touch. It's not that simple.

It's like something's been sucked out of the air

and spat out somewhere else.

Somewhere I can't see.

We do stupid poetry at school about loss and great aching pains in your heart, but it doesn't feel like that most of the time either.

It feels more like somebody has turned a big dial in an anti-clockwise direction and made all the colours of trees and sky and sea and bushes a bit less bright, like I'm seeing them through one of those revolting, yellow-brown net curtains that old people have in their front rooms.

There's no point trying to explain this to Mum and Dad.

They'll only start talking about counsellors and therapy and grief again which is v embarrassing and doesn't do any of us any good.

I only got them off my back before by promising to keep an anger diary, as one of the women counsellors suggested. And I didn't even keep that for the first year and a half, but just stared every night at the blank page and wondered why the words wouldn't come out, until one day I managed to write *groo* and all the rest sort of came from there. It does help me to scribble my thoughts in it from time to time.

But the sky still looks as though it's been drained of all the blue.

✳ ✳ ✳

Jay was a good brother until things went wrong.

That's why I miss him so much.

He was my favourite person next to Bindi.

I mean, yeah, don't get me wrong – sometimes I hated him. We fought and all that. Like brothers and sisters do. Sometimes he drove me mental with his arguing and teasing and winding me up about boys. And he knew just how to wrap Mum around his little finger. One flash of his lopsided grin, and she would melt like cheddar under a grill.

He wasn't so cheeky with Dad, though. Dad's quite scary when he loses his smile, folds his big tattooed arms and glowers over the top of his glasses.

Jay was just about the only person who would listen to my twelve-year-old rantings and take them seriously.

'You're my little sis,' he'd say, whenever I was upset or in trouble. 'Tell me who did this to you and I'll go smash their head in, if you like.'

Of course, he never did. He was gentle. He got upset if animals were mistreated, or if he saw anything on the news about cruelty to children or pets.

But Jay made me feel safe. It was us together against Mum and Dad. The Old Dudes, as he liked to call them. That's how it's supposed to be, right?

My brother listened to Indie rock music like you wouldn't believe. It was the main thing in his life, other than me. He always had a pair of headphones clamped on or a guitar slung round his neck. By the time he was fifteen he was playing in a band, and they were good. Really good. Record label interest and all that.

Jay had six electric guitars posing on metal stands around his bedroom. He saved up the money for them himself, bit by bit, doing summer jobs and cadging donations out of Mum when she was in a good mood. Watching Jay with his guitars was a bit like watching other people with their pets. He picked each of them up and checked them over, tuned them and returned them lovingly to their stands. He polished them, restrung them and ordered effects pedals to plug into them.

He loved a band called Muse, but mostly he

modelled himself on Richey from Manic Street Preachers.

I'd never heard of them, but Jay said they were a band from the 1990s whose lead guitarist had disappeared without trace, never to be seen again.

Jay copied Richey's hairstyle and even wore black eye make-up to imitate his look. His band covered all of Manic Street Preachers's songs, but he also wrote his own and they were brilliant.

But Jay didn't disappear because his idol did.

No.

Jay's disappearance wasn't an accident, either.

It was all because of me.

* * *

It's over two years since I saw my brother's face.

His bedroom isn't exactly left as a shrine, because Mum went in there and had a good old clear-up on one of her bad days, but all his posters are still on the wall and his CDs are lined up on their shelf over his bed. His clothes hang in the wardrobe and they still smell a bit of him: roll-up cigarettes, shower gel, mints and the late-night smell of pubs and gig venues.

On the day he went missing, he left everything

behind except his mobile.

All his things are still here.

His wallet, his clothes, his rucksack and his contact lenses.

His six guitars still sit around the room, waiting to be picked up and played.

I tried to play one once, but it made a noise like a dying cat when I switched it on and strummed a chord.

Sometimes I come in and give them a good polish, just the way that Jay used to.

It's kind of my way of staying in touch with him.

Wherever he is.

CHAPTER SIX

LILAH'S ANGER DIARY MARCH 25th
(Breakfast time)
ANGER LEVELS: **10/10**

It's Jay's birthday. He'd be eighteen today if he was living at home. He might be eighteen somewhere else. If he's still alive.

***

I ask Mum if I can stay off school, because I know I'm not going to be able to concentrate on dull things like Maths and Science.

'I don't think so, Lilah,' is all she says, but her voice is low and firm enough to have me sigh and stuff my schoolbooks into my bag.

She doesn't have any parties today, so she's going to use the morning to write a letter to Jay instead.

She wrote him one last birthday, too, and the one before that.

She's keeping them for when he comes home, so that she can show him how much he was missed.

Dad's working with the big cats today, but he's coming home early to have lunch with Mum and support her because it's the hardest day of the year for her, other than Christmas, which is pretty rubbish without Jay too, and the anniversary of the day he disappeared, which is probably the worst of all.

When he first went missing, I did that thing you do when you come back from a really cool holiday and it's a bit crap being back in the usual boring routine, so you think, *This time last week, I was still on holiday doing x or y.*

This time two weeks ago I was still on holiday doing x or y.

Except that I started to do the same thing about Jay.

The day he went missing I thought, *This time yesterday we were talking up in his bedroom.*

Well – arguing, more like. I try to not think about that last conversation too much.

And even three weeks after he went missing, I was still doing it. *This time a month ago he was still living with us, and everything was OK.*

Except it wasn't.

Not really.

∗ ∗ ∗

So I'm at school and in a foul mood.

I don't want to be here, and I can feel the familiar anger burning up in my throat and chest like acid.

Bindi's doing her best to cheer me up, but she's a bit distant this morning and I don't have the energy to ask her why, and I get told off in Maths for staring out of the window and watching the caretaker sweep the tennis courts and chewing my pen when I should be thinking about percentages.

Here's my take on percentages:

I'm eighty percent angry and twenty percent miserable. And that's on a good day.

Dad is sixty percent miserable and forty percent OK.

And Mum?

She's one hundred percent miserable.

All the time.

✳ ✳ ✳

I didn't get angry straight away.

For the first year after Jay disappeared, I was so shocked that I crept around not speaking to anybody and lying awake at night.

At school I stopped joining in with group activities and sat at the back of the class with my head lowered so that the teachers wouldn't pick on me.

That never works, right?

I learned that the hard way.

Teachers always pick on the people trying to hide at the back.

I lost count of the number of times I'd flush bright red and not be able to answer a question.

Bindi's grades went up and up and mine went down the opposite way, until she was at the top of the class and I was at the very bottom.

I didn't mind, though.

Bindi's the only person who has really got me through the last two years.

We've been friends forever.

Well, OK, not forever, but it feels like it.

I went round to her house the evening of the same day that Jay disappeared.

'He'll be back,' she said. 'He's probably just gone to get a bit of breathing space.'

Turns out she was wrong, of course. I mean, nobody needs to breathe away from their family for two years, do they? But I was glad that she said it.

She's nudging me right now.

'What?' I hiss back. The teacher is chalking up a load of complicated-looking symbols and shapes on the board.

I hate Maths.

My head doesn't work that way.

It doesn't do neat angles and lines and boxes and worked-out answers.

My head is a jumble of songs and clothes and animals and big red flashes of rage. All these things spin around in a random order. It can be quite tiring.

Bindi's brain works in a different way. She's tidy and organised and has great powers of concentration, like one cat trying to outstare another. But now she's not paying attention to the teacher, she's waving a bit of paper at me.

I snatch it and read it under my desk.

Adam's staring at you! it says, in her neat spider scrawl. *Maybe you've still got a chance with him. Why don't you ask him out on another date? Take your mind off things.*

I give my best sardonic snort at that.

As if going out with Band Boy is going to suddenly take away all my problems.

It's not going to bring Mum's smile back again, is it?

It's not going to get Dad to focus on me for a change, instead of worrying about his lions.

And it's not going to bring my brother home again.

I might, I scribble. *Cheers.*

But I'm way too embarrassed after what happened last time.

Bindi gives a self-satisfied smirk and a nod, like she's running a dating agency or something and has just nabbed a client. Then she turns her cat-eyes back towards the gibberish on the blackboard and picks up her calculator.

***

When I get in, I expect to see both my parents in the kitchen, but Dad's not there.

Mum's sitting in a pool of lamplight at the kitchen table, staring at a piece of paper. There's a plate with two half-eaten cream crackers and a wedge of cheddar next to it and a half-drunk glass of red wine.

'Where's Dad?' I ask. 'I thought he was supposed to be here today. Because of – you know. . .'

Mum looks up and gives me a wan smile. Her skin looks dry and tired and her blue eyes are small and watery. She's still got traces of greasy red make-up around her eyes from yesterday, when she had to be a clown for a group of seven-year-olds.

'Lazarus has injured his paw,' she says. 'Dad'll be a while yet.'

Lazarus is the biggest lion at Morley Zoo. Of course Dad gave him that weird biblical name. He's obsessed.

I sit down at the table with her and there's an awkward silence, the sort we've had a lot of over the last two years.

I look at Mum's wrinkled hand on the table and I wonder if I should hold it, but we stopped doing all that sort of thing ages ago, and now the only contact I ever have with my parents is when Dad gives me a brief head-kiss in the mornings before he heads off to the zoo.

'Did you do your letter?' I ask instead.

Stupid. I can see it there in front of her, complete with big blurry splodges where her tears have fallen.

Mum nods. She pushes the piece of paper towards me.

'You can read it if you like, love,' she says.

I shake my head in a panic.

Mum's written three of these letters since Jay went missing and I've not read a single one of them.

That's because, if I do, I'll remember that him not being here is all my fault.

Mum does her mind-reading thing.

'I've told you over and over,' she says. 'But I'm going to tell you again. What happened was not your fault. OK? You did the right thing.'

I give her a small smile because it's what she wants to see, but deep down I know that it's a lie.

The flame of anger starts to lick and flicker at my insides.

I want to kick something. Hard. Or do what I usually do when some well-meaning but annoying adult asks me how I am, or tries to tell me that things aren't my fault – go up to my bedroom, sit on the bed and bang the back of my head as hard as possible against the cold, white Artex wall until the anger just gets numbed away.

I make an excuse and leave the table to write what I can't say in my diary. I don't want to upset Mum.

Not today.

LILAH'S ANGER DIARY   MARCH 25th

ANGER LEVELS: 9/10

I should have done the wrong thing instead. If I'd done the wrong thing, then maybe, just maybe . . . Jay might still be here.

CHAPTER SEVEN

It's a hot summer's evening in July a few years ago. I'm lying face down on top of a canal boat with my hands propping up my chin and the toes of my plimsolls drumming on the hot metal roof.

Jay's lying next to me on his stomach too. He's just turned fifteen and discovered his passion for rock music. He's wearing tiny earphones and nodding his head up and down to the beat.

I've got a book but I'm bored with it.

Mum and Dad have gone off to one of their millions of canal-side pubs for the evening and left us a picnic and a bottle of lager shandy each as a treat, but Jay's just produced a bottle of cider from some hidden part of his luggage. So we're taking turns swigging from the bottle, and the cider is giving me a pleasant muzzy sort of feeling in my head, until the sky seems bluer and more vivid and the air brushing over my cheeks smells gorgeous – newly-cut grass and warm, swampy canal water mixed with the distant smell of scampi and chips from the pub.

I pull at his earphones.

'Hey, Liles, cut it out,' he says, but he's giving me his lazy grin from underneath his dark mop of hair.

When Mum and Dad go out, it's as if we enter our own little world. They go out a lot because of their weird jobs that take them out at strange times of the day and night, so often it's just Jay and me. Sometimes we don't speak, we do our own thing, but it's kind of a safe feeling knowing he's there next to me.

Tonight I want to chat, though.

I pull harder at his earphones, until he takes them out himself with a resigned sigh and flips over onto his back, staring up at the clouds.

'I'm knackered,' he says. 'All those bloody locks. Why can't the Old Dudes pick a canal without any?'

'I don't think there are many without locks,' I say. 'We could suggest a river next time.'

Mum and Dad have us leaping onto the banks

of the canal all day, running towards locks with big keys and pumping like fury at the gates until the water goes up or down and we can cruise into the lock for the long boring wait to get out the other side. By which time, we've had to leap off the boat yet again to swing open the heavy gates and let the boat through.

There's usually some sort of crisis.

This morning, I held the boat too tight in the lock and forgot to unwind the rope when the water drained down, so that the entire boat was suspended in mid-air like some weird, water-skimming aeroplane, and then when I let go of the rope in a panic, the boat smacked down onto the water and all the china in the kitchen slithered off the shelves and smashed on the floor.

The day before, a cow put its front legs on the boat and then got in a right state when it couldn't get them off again.

The day before that, we woke up to find that the boat had come loose from its moorings in the night and we'd drifted about a mile upstream and into the path of several oncoming boats.

But it's kind of fun. Mum screams and Dad tries to calm her down and we leap on and off the boat like demented frogs and eat a lot of chicken sandwiches and all in all, it's just being a normal mad happy family.

Except that we don't usually get this much attention from Mum and Dad.

Most of the time we're left to amuse ourselves.

It takes a holiday on a boat to kind of weld us together again.

Jay's flipped back over onto his front now and is observing me over the top of his shades.

'You're growing up, Liles,' he says.

I flush.

I'm still only twelve and haven't started wearing make-up and piercings yet. My hair's scraped back into a ponytail and my skin's all fresh and freckled and young-looking.

But I've had to go shopping for a first bra which is kind of embarrassing, and I don't really want to talk about my sore chest with Jay, so I look up at the bridge and point at a couple who are there snogging, oblivious to the world.

'Do you do that?' I say.

Jay glances up at the bridge and laughs, but doesn't answer.

Sometimes I think that there's a secret, dark

place growing bigger in my brother, where a load of things go on that little sisters don't understand. Yeah, sure, he tells me things that he doesn't tell Mum and Dad, but sometimes he seems vague and shy.

'Yuk,' I say. 'I am never going to kiss a boy EVER.'

Jay gives me a sideways look.

'You'll have them queuing up for you in a few years, Liles,' he says.

I make a face, and then whack him over the head with a cushion until he surrenders and goes down into the cabin to get our picnic.

The next day I have this weird, out-of-body-type experience.

We've been cruising down the canal all day, and now we've moored up and decided to eat inside tonight as there's a cold wind.

Mum's laid the tiny table that gets folded away at night to make way for our beds.

There's loads of good food – cold hard-boiled eggs, green salad, fresh, soft white rolls and a home-made chicken and ham pie from a shop we found earlier in the day.

Jay's already picking at a bowl of crisps, even

though Mum's trying to slap his hands away from it.

'Why do teenage boys get so hungry?' she says, but she's smiling.

We eat all the food, and then Dad draws the dark-red curtains in the tiny windows and puts on the lamps, and we sit round the table and play a very long and argumentative game of Scrabble. Jay's laughing his head off at Mum's pathetic attempts to come up with words that nobody's ever heard of, and it's as if one minute I'm there, part of it all, and the next I've floated up towards the low ceiling and I'm looking down at the four of us sitting below. I can see the parting in Mum's hair and the remnants of powdery grey dry shampoo on Dad's, the dark curls that smother Jay's head and the smoother, shinier hair on top of my own.

It's such a clear vision of a family. A happy family unit.

Unbreakable. Or so I thought

'I'm going to remember this,' I say, somewhere inside my head. 'Some day when I'm not so happy.'

I thought then that maybe I'd be a grey old lady when I remembered the scene on the boat.

How wrong can you be?

CHAPTER EIGHT

Sometimes I wish I'd been born a boy. Jay got away with just about everything when he was fifteen and still lived at home. He came in when he wanted, stayed out late, drank beer up in his bedroom, had his mates round for parties when Mum and Dad went away, rolled out of bed in the morning and straight into jeans and T-shirt before heading out at the weekend to chill with his band.

I'm not allowed to do any of that. I'm fifteen now, but the way Mum and Dad go on at me, you'd think I was about twelve. I'm not allowed to go out after dinner unless Mum has phoned the parents of whichever friend I'm visiting and checked that I'm not lying. I'm not allowed to have anybody over for sleepovers because Mum says her nerves are too fragile, and she can't cope with being deprived of her beauty sleep by our late-night chattering if she's got to pull bunnies out of hats for a children's party the next day.

I'm expected to do all my own washing too. Bindi thinks that is hilarious. Reeta does all the family's washing, and cooks, cleans and runs about after them, and still seems pretty happy. My mum goes on and on about how she spends too much time in the kitchen. 'I wasn't actually born at the kitchen sink, you know,' she says.

I don't answer. I'd only be rude, and I'm fed up of being angry and rude all the time, but the thing is, I can't seem to stop it. How do you stop being angry deep inside? I reckon I'll never stop.

Not until Jay comes home again.

CHAPTER NINE

It's after the boat holiday that Jay starts to change.

It's only little things at first.

I don't even really take much notice of them.

He's a bit more distant, like he's thinking about something he loved and lost. If I say something to him, it takes him a moment to focus on me before he can give me an answer. The old Jay was really quick and snappy and would throw a clever reply straight back.

He starts wearing more black and throws out all his old blue and white rugby shirts and khaki shorts that he used to wear when he was younger.

He stops taking showers.

He spends more and more time up in his bedroom, instead of chatting and strumming his guitar downstairs at the kitchen table like he used to, leaning back on the wooden chair, his curls dropping over his sharp, clever face and his foot tapping up and down on the kitchen lino.

'I never thought I'd say this,' says Mum, 'but I quite miss Jay playing his guitar in the kitchen.'

We laugh about it because it's all just normal adolescent stuff, we reckon.

He's a teenage boy, after all, and loads of girls at my school have brothers who are way weirder than Jay. Bindi's cousin is sixteen and obsessed with fish. He wants to be a marine biologist when he leaves school. Her aunt doesn't much care. Her main priority is to get him married off to a nice Indian girl so that she can have some grandchildren to spoil and cook for.

If I look back now at how Jay was then, I can almost chart the journey towards what happened, but at the time I just went along with whatever he did because I was his Liles, his baby sister, and I kind of adored him . . . when he wasn't pissing me off, as brothers do.

Later on, that boat holiday took on a sort of sad orange glow, as if it was the last time any of us were truly happy, as if we had been living in a protective bubble, and some big god with a sharp pin was hovering right above us, about to plunge it in.

* * *

It's six weeks after the holiday, and we're up in his bedroom with the door shut and his latest Manic Street Preachers album blaring out.

I'm lying on the bed watching Jay.

He's started straightening his hair over the last week or so. He's trying to make it look more like Richey from the Manics.

'I think it looked OK curly,' I offer from where I'm staring up at the old glow stars on his ceiling. Mum stuck them up there when he was a little boy, and despite Jay's best efforts at scraping them off, they're still there.

After he disappeared, I spent hours lying in there in the dark looking up at the little moon-shaped lights.

Stupid.

Like a load of stick-on planets could give me any answers.

Jay pulls the irons down over a section of his fringe until it flops against his pale forehead, dead black and straight. He's started to dye his hair too. The dark-brown curls that turned coppery-red in the sun have been replaced by this dead black gloss, the colour of the old vinyl LPs that he collects at record fairs and sometimes plays on an ancient record player of Dad's. He's wearing tight black jeans, grey plimsolls and a black long-sleeved top.

'Who asked you?' he says.

The tone of his voice catches me by surprise.

I sit upright and stare at him in the mirror.

'Sorry,' I say. 'I just liked your hair the way it was. But it's cool now too.'

Jay nods, unsmiling.

'How's it going at school, Liles?' he says, and I blather on in that twelve-year-old way about homework and teachers and two girls who are trying to bully me, and he makes 'hmm' noises from time to time, but I get the strangest feeling that he's just going through the motions. As if deep within him something's been switched off.

'Well, let me know if you want me to come in and beat anyone up,' he says, like he always does. But this time it doesn't seem like so much of a joke.

I get up and make for the door.

'Yeah,' I say. 'I will. How are things at school with you?'

Jay catches my eye in the mirror and then looks away.

'Most of them act like idiots,' is all he says, but I pick up on some hurt in his voice.

As I close the door, he whacks up the volume on his stereo and then starts to apply black eyeliner around the insides of his eyelids ready for band practice later.

I stand outside his bedroom door for a moment, feeling at a loss as to what to do next. I put my hand on the door handle as if to go back in, because I'd rather spend more time with Jay than talk to Dad about big cats for the rest of the evening, but something about the rawness of the music makes me stop.

It's the first time I feel it.

It's only a brief flash, but it cuts through all my childish thoughts and touches something deeper inside that throbs with shock, like a tongue running over a tooth that needs a filling.

It's loss, mixed with pain.

I shake my head to rid myself of the feeling.

I close myself up in my bedroom and write an English essay, but my heart's not really in it.

Jay's music stops at eight and he thunders downstairs and off to band rehearsal.

I watch him from behind my curtains.

His lanky, hunched figure walks with purpose down the road. He tosses his hair back every now and then before he becomes a little stick in the distance, but I watch for as long as I can.

Even after he's gone, I carry on staring down the street for a long time.

The house feels like the warmth's gone out of it when Jay's not around.

I go downstairs with a sigh and spend the evening talking to Dad, but I can't stop looking at the clock.

'Are you late for something?' says Dad. 'Because as far as I can remember, you're twelve, which means that the only thing left for you to do tonight is take a bath and go to bed. Right?'

In those days I hadn't yet come up with my Lilah-isms, so I just give him a mock-glare and then slope off upstairs.

Parents think they're so funny with all the

sarcasm stuff. As if they know everything in the world and they've got it all sorted out, and there's nothing that could ever happen that would shock or throw them off course, because they'd just carry on being those wise old parents.

But even they couldn't stop the bomb from going off in our house.

CHAPTER TEN

<u>LILAH'S ANGER DIARY</u> MARCH 26th

ANGER LEVELS: 11/10

(I know that's, like, really crap maths, but it's how I feel.)

Sometimes I hate Jay for making me like this.

I don't want to go to school today. If I see Adam Carter, I still flush with embarrassment and guilt. He's always been really nice to me, and what do I do? I come over like some mad psycho-witch from hell. Groo.

I feel really bad about upsetting everyone. But I can't seem to stop.

* * *

School's a bit of a nightmare.

Bindi seems distracted and not even all that interested in my problems.

Adam gives me a nice smile, but I reckon it's only a smile of pity, so I blush and turn away.

I get home to find Mum crying in the kitchen. Again.

Dad is in after tending to an injured lion, but he's got his throat bitten in the process and spends most of the evening disinfecting the wound with a big wad of cotton wool, while Mum tells him for the fifteen-millionth time how working with lions isn't really ideal if you want to live into happy old age and enjoy your pension.

'Lazarus is just a big pussy cat, really,' Dad says. This throws Mum into a state of violent agitation and she starts snapping and roaring and pacing up and down on the kitchen lino, a bit like Lazarus himself.

'I can't believe you just said that!' she yells.

'Well, at least I'm here for Lilah when she gets home from school,' Dad fires back. 'You're supposed be part-time, but I haven't noticed much difference. You're still never around.'

'Oh right,' Mum snaps. 'And I suppose you've never thought how difficult it is for me trying to entertain rooms full of kids when I'm so miserable that I'm starting to FRIGHTEN them now!'

They don't take a lot of notice when I came in all fired up with rage and in a boy-hating mood to beat all boy-hating moods.

Then Dad storms off to the pub. It's his once-weekly treat. He says it helps him let off steam about Jay.

Fine.

I don't need them fussing over me, anyway.

I'm used to being ignored.

* * *

'So, are you going to see him again?' Bindi's hissing from behind her hand.

It's the next day and we're in Biology.

There's a diagram of a tapeworm on the whiteboard in front of us, and the teacher's pointing at various segments of its revolting body with a stick, like she's some weird white-coated orchestra conductor.

'No I'm NOT,' I hiss back. 'And stop asking me!

You're doing my head in.'

Bindi stares at me with her mouth open. We never have 'words'.

'Lilah,' the teacher is saying. 'Perhaps, with your expert knowledge of tapeworms, you'd like to tell the class what I'm pointing at?'

The class titters at this.

I failed my last set of Biology exams after I drew a pair of glasses and a goofy grin on my tapeworm. The teachers were speechless when they marked it, apparently.

I got ten percent for that exam.

Big deal.

My brother's missing. I don't care that I graffitied all over a tapeworm.

What have tapeworms ever done for me?

'I don't give a crap, Miss,' I say.

The class groans. There are some stares of disbelief.

Adam Carter's avoiding my eye, but I see him shake his head from side to side, as if in slow motion.

'I've had it with you, May,' snaps the teacher. 'You can stay in at break and help me clean up this classroom.'

I sink down in my chair and bury my head in my hands.

I wish I could stop getting in trouble.

I wish I could stop being angry all the time.

It's cost me my friendship with Adam Carter, and now it even looks like it could threaten my friendship with Bindi, judging by the surly expression on her pretty face.

Why did you have to go, Jay? I scream inside my head. *Why?*

I'm on a downwards spiral.

Even Dad can't really control me any more.

'I find it ironic,' he says nearly every day. 'I can tell a twenty-stone lion what to do, no problem. But can I tame my own fifteen-year-old-daughter?'

It's what he calls a 'rhetorical question', so he's not actually inviting answers, but Mum's going to give him one, anyway.

'No,' she says. 'Our daughter is out of control.'

And even I can't argue with that.

82

Dad's obviously been thinking a bit more about the issue of me being untameable, because the next morning he announces that we are going to have a weekly Taming Lilah session, and that the issue is not up for discussion.

Great.

He books me in for a session after school tomorrow. God knows what he's going to do to me, but it's bound to be something he uses on the lions at Morley Zoo.

I hope he's not going to blow up my nose or throw me to the ground and leap on top of me.

Or shoot me.

Groo.

* * *

So I'm moping around on my own in the playground, watching a bunch of kids trying to kill each other and the dark rain clouds gathering over the high red roof of my school and all the white sheets on the washing lines of the houses that back onto our school fluttering and flipping over in the wind, and then Adam Carter's there at my elbow, as if he was summoned by a magic lamp or something.

'I'm busy,' I say.

Talk about stupid comments. But I don't want to talk to him right now.

'No you're not,' he says in an even, calm way. He sits on the wall next to me. I get a whiff of his leather jacket and my heart flips in pain. 'It's break-time.'

'It's possible to be busy in your head, idiot,' I say.

That's true, in fact.

If I had an 'engaged' red light, like you get on train toilets, on the outside of my head, I'd switch it on right now.

I've been thinking about Jay.

Not the Jay who started to change, but the one who used to play with me when we were younger.

It's like we were both these little paper men cut out of the same sheet or something.

His sense of humour was my sense of humour.

It was all so easy. We lived in this little world of our own making. Same toys, same games, same favourite foods, same words that made us splutter with laughter.

We'd spend hours recording tracks from the Top Forty and discussing them. Sometimes Jay would let me have a go on his guitar. He placed his fingers over mine on the strings, and helped me strum enough chords to be able to play 'Mull of Kintyre', an old song that always had us falling about in hysterics.

He smelled familiar. His room did too. Sweat and dirty plates and musty old copies of NME, his favourite music mag.

I can't go in his bedroom too often now. Most of the smell's gone, replaced by Mum's cleaning fluids and the smell of fabric conditioner. She's put the stack of NMEs inside the sliding yellow wardrobe, underneath his clothes.

When he went missing, Mum put his keys, wallet, passport, watch and iPod in a box, after the police had finished with them.

'For when he comes back,' she said.

I don't look in the box. I don't touch his stuff. I don't often go into his room. I only polish the guitars from time to time but I can't bear to stay in there for more than a few minutes.

The silence in there is unbearable. It grows and threatens to eat me if I stay too long.

I miss our chats.

I thought I'd always have him there to talk to.

I always thought that I'd go right through life with my big brother there to support me.

That's what's supposed to happen.

Isn't it?

***

'I'm sorry about the other night, Lilah,' says Adam, still in an even tone.

I glance sideways.

It's hard staying cross with him for long.

He smells so gorgeous. Looks pretty good, too. He's in uniform, of course, but the tie's done up loose like Pete Doherty or something, and his hair's been gelled up at the front. Even in uniform he still looks like a rock star.

'It was my fault,' I say. 'I guess I thought – oh crap, this is embarrassing – I guess I thought that maybe you wanted to be more than a friend. I can't believe I'm saying this.'

I feel my face going hot, so I twist my head in the other direction and pretend to watch the third years trying to play tennis in a stiff wind. Green Slazenger balls are spinning all over the place.

One of them comes towards me, so I trap it

underneath my shoe and make a great play of rolling it back and forth.

'Oy!' shouts a small girl with frizzy black hair on the other side of the netting. 'Can we have our ball back, if it's not TOO much trouble?'

Adam rescues it from underneath my foot and lobs it back at her.

Then he stands in front of me and glowers down at me with a very old look in his eyes.

'I used to think about asking you out, yeah?' he says. 'But over the last year you've got really angry, and it freaks me out.'

I nod, and stare down at my black leather T-bar shoes. We all have to wear revolting girly shoes at this school. I feel about six.

'Sorry,' I say in a quiet voice.

'It's OK,' says Adam. 'I know why you're angry, of course. It's not your fault.'

I know he's right. But I can't stop the anger rising up. I can even feel bits of it now, even though he's made me feel small and sad and stupid.

It just won't go away.

The hideous day gets even worse. I'm just dragging my feet down the school corridor towards double Latin, and I see a nightmare vision coming towards me in the shape of my MOTHER in full clown costume and curly wig. She's clutching a set of yellow juggling balls and a selection of cricket bats and hoops.

'Oh, hello, darling!' she says. 'You'll never guess who's been asked to speak to the fourth years about careers in entertainment.'

'No,' I say, darting looks up and down the corridor to make sure none of my class are watching. 'I couldn't possibly guess.'

Mum scowls at my sarcasm, but then her face lights up again. Or at least, it tries to, underneath the big, sad, down-turned clown mouth that she's spent all morning painting on.

'I'm stepping in at short notice,' she says. 'They were supposed to be having a talk from the head of Film Studies at the local college, but he's got a cold, so the head rang me up instead.'

'Great,' I say. 'And now I must go, before I die of embarrassment.'

Oh, *groo*. Too late. Here's Amelie Warner and her bunch of witch-mates all giggling and shoving past us like a big, wriggling monster with six heads.

I'd been feeling kind of guilty about shoving Amelie off her chair and I'd been rehearsing a grudging apology in my head, but when I see her horrible blonde curls bouncing around her pointy chin, and her eyes all lit up with spite, I feel a new surge of anger take hold of me.

'Just ignore them,' says Mum. 'They're jealous. Their parents probably wear grey suits and work as accountants.'

Sounds like bliss to me. I allow myself a big huffy sigh at this untouchable vision of normality. A vision I can only dream of.

Then I watch my mother the clown open the door into the classroom next to us, and listen to the children erupt in stunned laughter as she begins to flip the yellow balls in the air and shout out of her big, painted red mouth.

Is this hideous day ever going to end?

Adam walks me home after school.

'So I guess we can stay mates, right?' I say in a nervous voice.

I'm trying hard not to upset him or be angry.

'For now,' says Adam. 'See how things go, yeah?'

That's kind of fair, so I stick out my hand in a businesslike way and he gives a snort of laughter and then shakes it.

'Seriously, though, Lilah,' he says. 'Have you ever thought of seeing somebody?'

'What – you mean a date?' I say, confused.

Adam sighs.

'I mean about your anger,' he says. 'There must be people who can help you.'

It's my turn to sigh. In the weeks and months after Jay disappeared a whole army of do-gooding counsellors and therapists descended on our little house after my mum got it in her head that I was having some sort of breakdown, and despite their best efforts to make me talk and 'let it all out', I refused to speak to any of them.

'No good,' I say. 'Been there, bought the T-shirt, worn the T-shirt, ripped it off and sent it to Oxfam.'

Adam gives another snort.

'You're mental, May,' he says. 'But I think that's why I like you.'

I smile, but I'm thinking about what he said about getting help.

The thing is, I know that there's only one

thing that will help me stop being angry.

And that one thing just never seems to happen.

I need Jay to come home.

But even if he did . . . would he ever forgive me?

CHAPTER ELEVEN

Jay's losing weight.

He says it's because he's not been bothering to eat anything much at band practice, and it's true, when I once went to watch them rehearse, they spent the whole evening existing on cans of lager and a bag of red liquorice.

But Mum's getting a bit worried about him.

'He doesn't talk to me any more,' she says to me when we're washing up together at the sink. 'And when he does, it's only in words of one syllable.'

I scrunch my tea towel into a glass and squeak it around inside until it's smudge-free and shiny.

'Maybe he's just being a typical teenage boy?' I offer. 'And to be fair, Mum, you're not exactly here very much, are you?'

Mum flushes, and turns back to her washing-up.

'You're too young to know what you're talking about,' she snaps. 'Somebody has to pay the bills around here.'

I shrink away from her. I'm only twelve, going on thirteen. And I wasn't at all moody or angry back in those days. I was a sunny child, or so my parents were always saying.

'She's got a lovely sunny nature, our Lilah,' they'd say to anybody within earshot, and then whoever it was would turn around and stare at me with a sort of bemused fondness, and I'd go all embarrassed and squirmy.

'I don't know,' sighs Mum. 'You never know how your children are going to turn out. I mean, you're no trouble. Not yet. But Jay was a lovely little boy. Really sweet. And now he just bites my head off if I ask him a question.'

I carry on wiping the plates dry and I don't

say anything, but I'm thinking that I actually know exactly how Mum is feeling, because Jay's started being a bit weird with me too. And my brother being snappy with me is the most horrid and unexpected thing that's ever happened, and it's too upsetting to talk about, so I just carry it around inside me like a big, mould-covered, heavy lump of rock that won't go away.

'Go and talk to him, Lilah,' says Mum. 'I can finish the drying-up. He always seems to prefer talking to you.'

She doesn't sound bitter when she says this, just a little lost and wistful.

I don't really want to go and disturb Jay and risk getting snapped at, but I'm still at that age where I obey my parents, so I put down my plate and go upstairs.

Jay's bedroom door is shut, as usual, but there's no music pumping out, which is kind of unusual, so I give a soft tap on the door and then hover in the hallway with my ear pressed to the wood.

There's a rustling, shifting sort of noise, and then Jay pads over to the door in socks and opens it.

'Not now, Liles,' he says.

His face is pale, and you can see his cheekbones

where the weight's come off his face. There's a stench coming out of the room behind him. Sweat, stale air and something else. Something I don't know, but it's sweet and sour all at once and strong enough to make me cough and back away.

'Are you ill?' I say, because he doesn't look very well. Jay used to have ruddy cheeks and a glow about him underneath the thick brown curly hair.

Now his face is stripped of all pinkness and his hair is dead straight and jet-black.

'I'm fine, Liles,' he says. 'I don't feel much like talking, though. Sorry. Maybe tomorrow?'

He shuts the door in my face, gently, but in a way that doesn't invite me to push it open again.

The smell hangs around in the corridor for a moment.

I put my ear to the door again and listen. I can't hear a thing.

Maybe he's gone to bed.

I go down the hall to my own room and lie on my pink duvet and stare up at my own glow stars for a bit, and then I dig out my homework and do it at the desk, all the time listening for any signs of life in the bedroom next door.

Just after I've gone to bed, I hear Jay creep out

of his room and down the stairs, and then there's the slam of the front door and a shout of protest from Mum and the sound of her and Dad talking in low urgent voices, but I can't work out what they're saying.

Jay doesn't come home at all that night.

CHAPTER TWELVE

LILAH'S ANGER DIARY   MARCH 29th (Teatime)
ANGER LEVELS: 6/10
An Improvement!

Phew. Adam Carter still likes me. Shame it's only as a mate, though.

And Bindi still looks like she wants to kill me. I wish she'd give me one of her wet-eyed smiles. I miss her. She's got quite friendly with Adam now. I think she feels sorry for him.

* * *

It's the evening after I've had the chat with Adam at school, and I've come home not exactly full of joy, but feeling a bit better now that we've agreed to be mates. I go upstairs to write in my diary and things feel at least a bit better.

I've still got a lot of sucking-up to do to Bindi, though. She didn't even say goodbye to me after school, and I don't get it. To add to my feelings of doom, I saw her making a special effort to be nice to Adam Carter, so now I feel even more horrible.

I only got her to stay by the phone for one evening. I mean, I didn't ask her to commit murder or anything, did I? But she's gone all sulky and quiet on me, so I guess I've got to buy her a present or something, and I'm just thinking about what to get her as I close my diary, when Dad comes in and announces that it's time for Taming Lilah, Session One.

'OK,' I say. I know when I'm beaten. Dad's rolled up his shirtsleeves to reveal his tattoos and put on his scariest black glasses. He's got a no-nonsense vibe coming off him. I can kind of see why the lions and tigers do whatever he says.

'Right,' he says, all business-like. 'Lions get angry. They need a release for their anger, kind of like you do. So I'm going to make you angry and then we're going for a run down the street. OK?'

I roll my eyes and cast a longing look at my bedroom door, but Dad's blocking it.

'So,' he says. 'How ARE you, Lilah? Tell me how you are.'

Dad has somehow picked up on the fact that I hate this question, and now he's using it to taunt me, like waving a stick in front of an angry tiger.

I'm not going to give in yet, though.

'Fine,' I say, with a big bright smile. 'I am absolutely fine. As fine as the finest person in Fineland.'

Dad gives a knowing nod.

'So there's nothing bothering you, then?' he says. 'That's great. So you're absolutely thrilled that your brother has gone missing, your school life is suffering, your best friend is fed up with you, and you hate being at home with your screwed-up parents, right?'

'Right,' I say, but my voice has faltered just a tiny bit, and Dad pounces on this as if *he* were the lion and I've just thrown a tasty piece of dead deer into the enclosure.

'Life just couldn't be better for you, could it?' he continues. 'In fact, I'm quite envious. You get all your meals here for free, your rent paid, while Mum and

I have to go out and earn loads of money so that you can sit about doing nothing and moaning about silly little things. Wish I was you!'

Damn. It's starting to work. I've got an itchy feeling going up my legs, and they're all hot and stuck together. Dad's got a really irritating smarmy grin on his face, and just looking at him is starting to annoy me now.

'Don't,' I mutter. 'I don't want to play this any more. It was a stupid idea.'

'Pardon?' says Dad. 'Speak up. I can't hear you.'

I flip my chin up and glare at him.

'I SAID, I don't want to play any more!' I shout back at him.

Dad's eyes begin to glint and spark.

'That's more like it!' he says. 'Feeling a bit angry, are we? Losing our temper a bit, are we?'

I'm seeing great big sheets of red in front of my eyes.

I swear that a *growl* escapes from my mouth! I hope I'm not actually turning into a lion.

'That's it,' says Dad. He's enjoying himself. 'Just let it out, Lilah. Scream if you want. Howl. Hit me. I don't really care. I can take it.'

I lunge towards him but I stop just at the last

moment because there's something deep and stern and kind in his eyes, and it reminds me that this is Dad and that he's quite scary.

Instead, I turn to the wall and start to kick it with my foot. Hard.

Water rushes into my eyes and the bones in my ankle ache and throb, but I can't seem to stop kicking.

Dad comes over and pulls me away from the wall.

'OK,' he says again. 'Downstairs. Out of the front door. Run up and down the street three times, as fast as you can. I'll race you, right?'

I don't know what he's doing to me, but I find myself obeying and running downstairs and down the hall, straight out of the front door and along the pavement, with my trainers pounding on the ground and the night air rushing past me in cold draughts and my breath coming all jagged and short and painful as I run my anger away. Dad runs along next to me, super-fit and fast, and my body feels so cold and breathless and *alive* that for once I don't think about Jay at all. I just focus on what I'm doing, and Dad keeps me going until I can't run any longer, and I collapse in a heap over our front wall.

'Good girl,' he says, handing me a bottle of water. 'How do you feel?'

I sit up, still panting, and pour the water over my head.

We sit together on the wall, and it's really weird, because I don't feel so angry any more.

A bit of me is still cross at the way he's bossing me about and making me leg it up and down our street in full view of all the neighbours, but there's all this buzzy adrenalin pumping around my head, and it feels clear and cool and good, and I don't feel like I want to kick anything any more.

Not that I'm going to tell Dad that.

Not yet.

'I feel OK,' I say in a small voice. 'But I think I need to go to bed now. You've worn me out.'

Dad gives a knowing smile and nudges me gently with his elbow. I very nearly turn round and smile at him, but I just manage to keep it under control.

'We'll try it again soon,' he says. 'Session Two. You in?'

I give a deep sigh and get up from the wall.

'Yeah,' I say. 'If it makes you happy, I'm in.'

The peace in our household doesn't last long.

I'm upstairs surfing Accessorize and deciding which bracelets to order online for Bindi, and then I freeze with my hands over the keys, because my parents have exploded into yet another argument downstairs and I can't concentrate. I creep down the stairs and sit on the bottom step.

'You don't even talk about Jay any more!' Mum is screaming. She's still got half a clown outfit on, which is kind of bizarre as she's taken off the wig and her normal, sensible, short Princess Di hair looks really odd above the big white ruff, red clown boots and white suit with big red buttons up it.

'He might as well not exist. All you care about is your bloody lions!'

Dad is sitting at the kitchen table with his arms folded over his head, perhaps to field off the imaginary bullets coming from Mum's direction, but at this, he stares up at her with shock in his tired blue eyes.

'You're talking rubbish, Rachel,' he says. His voice is low and cracks when he says Mum's name. 'Of course I think about him. Every day. I just don't go on about it like you do.'

Mum sees me sitting in the hall and lets out a big sigh. I watch her deflate and come towards me with her frilly arms outstretched.

'Don't,' I say, dodging the embrace. 'I'm so not in the mood for being groped by a clown.'

'Oh, so *you're* going to start on me now, are you?' says Mum, her voice going all wobbly. 'That's right. I forgot that you always side with your father. Well, just go ahead, both of you. Just lay into me like you always do.'

She stalks back into the kitchen and turns her back to us at the sink, throwing cups and plates into the soapy water.

Dad gets up and rubs his palms over his eyes. He glances at my mum's rigid back and then at my sulky face, and he throws his hands up like he's surrendering, and slams out of the house to go to the pub.

I watch my mother's back for a couple of moments and I think that now would be a good time for her to turn round and calm down, and then maybe, just maybe, I could tell her that I miss Jay too, and that they're not the only ones who feel screwed up and messed about and emotionally wrecked. And that I'm so angry most of the time from bottling all this stuff up that I give myself ice-cream headaches. But she doesn't turn round, even though she knows

I'm still there, and the tension hovers between us like some sort of giant angry dragonfly, so I stomp upstairs and go back online instead.

I crank up Planet Rock on my digital radio and I order Bindi an armful of jangly blue bracelets because she likes that sort of thing, and then I go onto my page on Facebook and look at all the boring, non-important things that my friends have been getting up to. And then I notice that I've got a message in my inbox, so I click on it to see who's invited me to some ridiculous event in Milton Keynes or something, because that's what it usually is, and instead there's a message from somebody who looks a bit familiar. And when I open up the message, the chair seems to buckle underneath me, and I lurch to one side and clutch the desk while my head swims and buzzes.

The message is from one of Jay's band mates.

Don't get your hopes up, it begins. *But I had a missed call on my phone last night. And, the thing is – it's from Jay's number. I tried to call back, but it just went to voicemail. I left a message anyway.*

I'm shaking so much that I have to get up and go and lie on the bed for a moment.

I hug my knees and rock back and forth, and I think about the last two years, and about my parents screaming at each other, and about all the times we went out looking for Jay, and about the huge police search just after he went missing, and the feature they did on television about missing people.

Then I get up and read the Facebook message again, just in case I've imagined it. But it's still there, so I go downstairs to where my mother is standing at the sink with her shoulders looking sad in the weird clown outfit, and I stand in the middle of the kitchen for a moment because I just don't know how to say what I've just read without making her scream, or faint, or get her hopes up.

Mum turns around with a start.

'Didn't realise you were there,' she said. 'Sorry about before. I'm just feeling a bit sad today. Somebody at one of my parties said that I was one of the most miserable children's entertainers they had ever seen, and it kind of upset me. I used to be really good. Never mind. I'll make us a hot chocolate in a moment, if you like. I've even got marshmallows.'

Then she takes a closer look at my ghostly-white face, and she puts down the plate she's holding and grips me by the shoulders.

'You're frightening me,' she says. 'Lilah. What is it?'

I can't speak. I knew this would happen, so I've printed out a copy of the email.

I pass it to her. Then I catch my mother by the elbow just before she falls.

CHAPTER THIRTEEN

Mum rings Dad at the pub on his mobile and we go straight to the police with the email.

All three of us, even though it's now getting on for eleven o'clock at night.

Dad drives. He keeps glancing anxiously at Mum, who's as pale as death and gripping onto the door handle like she's going to break every time Dad takes a sharp corner.

Dad's teeth are gritted and he's muttering to himself as he navigates the large roundabouts.

I'm sitting in the back seat wrapped in a winter

coat, even though it's a mild spring night. I can't seem to stop shivering and my bones feel damp.

None of us speak.

We all want to say the same thing, but it's like if we let the words out it will jinx it, and then we'll be back to square one.

I think it, though, all the way to the station.

He could still be alive.

CHAPTER FOURTEEN

The first time Jay stays out all night, Mum sits in the kitchen in the dark with a cold cup of tea in front of her, and she waits.

She's still waiting in the early hours of the morning when I stagger downstairs for a drink, because I've woken up all stuck to the sheets in the sunshine streaming through my window.

'What are you doing?' I say. I'm kind of stupid first thing in the morning. I mean, it's obvious what she's doing. She's sitting at the table chewing her fingernails and staring towards the clock and then at the front door.

'Lilah, look at the state of you,' says Mum.

I glance into the wooden-framed mirror that hangs over the kitchen dresser. Yeah, I do look a bit of a mess. But then, I'm not yet thirteen, so I don't much care that my hair's sticking up on one side and there are yellow crusts of sleep stuck in the corners of my eyes. My feet are bare and my blue stripy pyjama trousers are starting to fall down around my not-yet-developed hips.

I pull two soft white squares of bread from a packet and stick them into the toaster.

'Do you want any?' I say.

Mum smiles, and shakes her head.

'Couldn't eat a thing,' she says. She watches as I plunge my knife into a jar of gloopy cherry jam and then smother the toast with it.

'That's expensive, make it last,' she says, like she's on autopilot, but she's looking towards the front door again.

'Where's Dad?' I say, stuffing soggy toast into my mouth. It's Saturday morning and he's usually at home doing the garden or compiling some sort of complicated meat dish for dinner later on.

'Shyama has gone into labour,' says Mum. 'He could be some time.'

I roll my eyes. Shyama is one of the lionesses at Morley Zoo. Dad's looked after her ever since she was a tiny cub with big floppy paws and a tendency to fall over and have to be nudged back up again by her mother.

'And where's Jay?' I say, all casual.

I know full well that he didn't come home last night.

I was up listening for him half the night.

Missing the sound of Manic Street Preachers through the wall.

Missing our chats. We never seem to have them any more.

'I'm losing my big brother,' I say, more to myself than Mum, but she hears and gives me a sharp look.

'Why would you say that?'

I shrug, and pour hot water into a mug with a teabag in it.

'Dunno,' I say. 'Just feels like it sometimes.'

Mum's giving me her full attention now.

'He's growing up, that's all,' she says. 'You can't expect him to want to play with you, like when you were both little. He's probably got girls on his mind now that he's nearly sixteen.'

It's my turn to give *her* a sharp look.

Jay's never mentioned girls. I've never seen him hang out with any either. I don't much like the idea of him confiding in other girls.

He's supposed to confide in me.

'Don't think so,' I say, but Mum's getting up and stretching. She's got dark rings beneath her eyes and her blonde hair is sticking up in short peaks where she's run her hands through it all night.

'I think I'd better stay at home today and ask Jenny to fill in for me,' she says. Jenny is Mum's one member of staff. She does the children's entertaining when Mum can't make it. 'I can't concentrate on anything until he comes home.'

She goes upstairs for a shower, and I gulp my tea and flick through a magazine at the kitchen table, like I've taken Mum's place and now it's me who's waiting for Jay to get home.

About two hours later, Mum's outside pruning pots of petunias to try and keep herself from panicking, and I've had a bath and come downstairs to do homework at the kitchen table, when there's a very quiet click at the front door and a key turns in the lock in a way which makes me think that the person turning it doesn't want to be seen or heard. So I get up and go and stand in the hall with my hands on my hips like an angry parent.

Jay jumps when he sees me standing there.

'Jeez, Liles, you nearly gave me a heart attack,' he says.

He looks dreadful.

His face is chalk-white and his hair has stopped being shiny and flippy and just lies across his pale forehead in dank, black, greasy strands. His eyes are empty and staring, and his black jeans are stained with something white.

There's that smell coming off him. I can't work out what it is, except that it doesn't smell like Jay.

'Don't worry, Mum's in the garden,' I say. 'But she's been up all night waiting for you.'

Jay shakes his head.

'Christ,' he says. 'They treat me like a little kid. That's when they can be bothered to actually stay in the house for more than an hour.'

'Maybe they worry because you don't tell them where you're going,' I suggest, but it's the wrong thing to say.

Jay pushes past me and bolts upstairs like a crazed black antelope or something.

'Jay!' I call after him. 'Do you want some breakfast?'

There's no reply.

He looks like he hasn't eaten for a week.

I stand in the kitchen feeling like a stupid little sister, and then Mum comes in and takes one look at my face and rushes upstairs, and there's one hell of a row, which ends with Dad being hauled out of Morley Zoo and summoned home with a face like an angry lion. And there's a 'family conference', which is dreadful, because Jay won't speak and just sits sunk in his chair with his hair falling over his face, and I feel like a spare part and can't speak either. And Mum and Dad just go on and on firing endless questions at Jay, with their voices getting higher and more hysterical, and he won't answer any of them.

That evening he stays up in his room.

Mum fiddles around with her uneaten spaghetti, winding strings of meaty pasta around her fork and then letting them unravel again in an anti-clockwise direction, until Dad reaches out, takes her fork and puts it on her plate, like she's a little child.

'Lilah,' he says.

Uh-oh. I know what's coming, and I don't like it.

'We need to know what Jay's going through,' he says. 'Obviously something is wrong. But he won't talk to us. Maybe he'll talk to you?'

I'm peeling the lid off a raspberry yoghurt, but I look up at that.

'He doesn't really talk to me either, any more,' I say. 'Not about anything important, anyway.'

'But you used to be so close,' says Mum. Her eyes are wet with tears. 'Won't you at least try?'

I put my yoghurt down uneaten and scrape back my chair.

'I'll try,' I say. 'But he's probably just going to yell at me.'

Jay doesn't yell at me.

He doesn't get the chance.

I go up to his room and this time, for some reason, I decide not to knock.

There's a part of me that's already starting to feel angry.

I'm not an angry child yet, so it's like a baby alien has just set up home in my stomach and started waving his arms and legs about. It feels strange.

I'm thinking about Mum's sad face and Dad having to leave a pregnant lioness about to give birth to lots of helpless little baby lion cubs, and about how every weekend is now dominated by us all worrying about what Jay's going to do or not do, and a little part of me is stirring up and feeling vivid and alive with anger. And it's wiping out all the good memories of the holiday on the boat and our childhood and all the games we used to play. So I don't even think of knocking politely on my brother's door, I just grip the handle and barge in.

It takes my eyes a moment to adjust to the gloom.

There's music blaring out and the window is shut, so the room stinks.

Jay's on the floor with his back up against the bed and his head drooping down towards his chest, and when I come in he kind of looks up, but as if in slow motion, and his eyes are frowning at me like he doesn't recognise me. And then he speaks in a voice that sounds as if he's drunk about twenty cans of lager, and he says, 'Get the hell out of my bedroom, little girl.' His voice is low and menacing, like the rumble of a train in the distance that's about to speed up and mow me down, so I start to back towards the door, but by then it's too late, and I've already seen it.

There's a tin on his lap, and some sort of needle lying next to him, and Jay's got a thin, black band pulled tight around his soft, white arm.

I've seen people doing it on television.

I know what it is.

'You tell Mum and Dad, you're dead,' says my brother in this new voice I don't recognise. 'Got it?'

I stumble out of the room backwards.

And I spend the night alone in my room.

CHAPTER
FIFTEEN

When we go and report the strange call from Jay's phone, the police aren't very helpful or sympathetic.

'Don't get your hopes up,' they say. 'We'll trace the call, but to be honest, anybody could have that mobile and be making calls on it.'

'But why would they call somebody from Jay's band, unless they were Jay?' says Mum. 'We've got to have some hope. It's been over two years,' she says, more to herself than to us.

She's holding my hand, but her nails are digging into my palm and her wedding ring is cutting into the side of my finger.

'You'd be surprised how many idiots there are out there, Mrs May,' says one of the policemen, a young guy with dark hair and serious brown eyes. He eyes my mother's weird clown costume as he speaks. 'Some people will do anything when they're bored.'

We drive home again in silence.

The tense air in the car has gone, to be replaced by a big deflated feeling, like we've all been blown up and popped with a giant pin.

'This sucks,' I mutter from the back seat, where I'm slumped against the window.

'Yes, Lilah, thank you for putting it so eloquently, as usual,' says Dad with a huge sigh. He's driving as if he can't be bothered, tipping the wheel back and forth with two fingers and leaning right back against the headrest.

I scowl in the dark, even though they can't see me, and mutter '*Seagullvians*,' to myself.

'Well, sorry you're left with your horrid daughter when all you want is your lovely son,' I say, although I know I shouldn't.

I can't help myself sometimes.

The anger just kind of takes hold of me and bursts out of my mouth, even if I press my lips really hard together.

'You're obviously going through your Terrible Teens,' says Mum. Her voice is broken and thick with tears. 'Jay was going through them as well, Lilah. I'm not saying he was perfect. Far from it.'

'Yeah,' I mutter, from where I've sunk down into my coat so that only my eyes are peering out. 'Whatever.'

Mum sighs and blows her nose. She hates my over-use of slang expressions from American chat shows.

The thing is, she's right. Jay was a nightmare just before he went missing. But now that's all been brushed aside because all we want is for him to come home. Whereas I'm still at home, still getting told off and bossed about and ordered to do homework and tidy my room, and I've got no freedom to go out at night now, thanks to my lovely big brother and his, like, *great* idea of going missing for two years.

When we get home, Dad goes upstairs to his computer, Mum locks herself in the bedroom and sticks her yoga music on and I lie on my bed and stare up at the glow stars for hours. I decide that I'm going to go mad if I don't speak to somebody, so I think about Bindi and then realise it's half past midnight and way too late for her to still be up. So I reach for my mobile and dial another number.

Adam answers the phone straight away, like he was holding it in his hand.

'Hey, Lilah. Wassup?'

I can't speak for a moment.

It's because his voice is deep and kind, even after our embarrassing non-date the other week. And I don't hear a lot of that at home at the moment, so whenever anybody's kind to me I start filling up with pathetic girly tears that won't fall down my face, and I feel about six years old.

'Lilah?' says Adam. 'Are you still there?'

I nod, which is stupid because he can't see me.

'Hi,' I manage, in a tiny whisper. 'Tell me what you're doing.'

Most people would think this weird, but Adam is used to my weirdness.

'Well,' he says, and I can picture him glancing around his bedroom. 'Before I answered this call, I was texting a mate. Before that, I was listening to the new Killers album on iTunes. And before that, I was stuffing a doughnut down my gob, and trying to do logarithms. How about you?'

'Mmm, you know,' I manage. 'Went down to

the police station. Somebody made a call from Jay's mobile. But they don't reckon it was him.'

I can tell by the silence that Adam's shocked.

'Shit, Lilah,' he says in the end. 'I'm so sorry. That must have brought it all back again.'

I'm silent again for a moment. The thing is, nothing ever brings it all back again, because it never went away in the first place.

I can't ever stop thinking about Jay.

And how it was entirely my fault.

LILAH'S ANGER DIARY   MARCH 30th
(Middle of the night so can't write much)
ANGER LEVELS: 4/10

I'm too sad to be angry.

* * *

The police call us the next day.

They've traced Jay's phone. Some strange bloke had found it in the street and had pressed a dialled number by mistake.

Mum's white with disappointment and Dad's pacing up and down in the kitchen in the manner of one of his lions.

I'm off school for a day because none of us slept a wink the night before.

'But I don't understand,' says Dad. 'Why would his phone end up in the street?'

Mum and I are silent.

Whatever the reason, it doesn't sound like something we'd want to know about.

CHAPTER SIXTEEN

Dad comes upstairs for another Taming Lilah session on a Thursday after school.

I'm already feeling pretty cross, because although Bindi liked her bangles, our friendship is still all cautious and nervy and not like it was before, and I see her whispering with Adam Carter sometimes during break, and I just know that they are discussing me and how annoying I am, and when I see them with their heads bent close together, I go all shivery and get a big pang deep in my stomach.

So I'm up in my bedroom trying to get lost in schoolwork, but as always there's this bad feeling right at the middle of everything I do, like the black bit you have to scrape out from the middle of a clean white potato. I just can't shift it.

Dad taps on my door and comes in without bothering to wait for my reply.

He's wearing a thick black jacket, which is a bit odd, as our house is heated up like a tropical greenhouse due to Mum's inability to tolerate any cold weather at all.

'How ARE you?' he begins. I poke my tongue out at him and we both laugh a little bit, but then I remember the afternoon I've just had at school and I begin to bang the back of my head against the wall, not really all that hard, but just enough to show Dad that I'm not at my best.

'That bad, huh?' says Dad. He comes over and sits on the foot of the bed.

'Well,' he says. 'When the big boys at the zoo get angry, there are a number of things we try. Firstly there's exercise, like you did last time. And secondly we use something called "the distraction method".'

I give him a mournful look.

'I'm so not in the mood for being distracted,' I say. 'And if you're about to suggest that we play a board game, then forget it.'

My family have this gross love of playing games. I hate them. They're not called 'bored games' for nothing. Just the tap-tap of the little plastic pieces around the board is enough to get my anger prickles starting off again.

'It depends what the distraction is, surely?' says Dad. He's got a worrying smirk on his face, like he knows something I don't.

But I'm kind of interested now, and I've stopped banging my head on the wall.

'What?' I say. 'Could you just tell me, please? I can't cope with all this mystery stuff.'

Dad puts his hand inside his odd black puffy jacket and pulls something out.

'Oh!' I say. My eyes are wide as frisbees.

Dad passes it into my trembling hands.

Two very big brown eyes look up at me, and a small pink tongue comes out and starts to pant.

'He's yours,' says Dad. 'But there are two conditions. Number one, you don't ever, ever take out your anger on this puppy. OK?'

'Of course,' I say. I've melted into a pile of slush

in the corner of the duvet. I can't stop gazing down at the bundle of golden fur in my arms.

'And number two,' says Dad, 'when you get angry, you take this little animal for a good run. That way, he gets his exercise and you get to feel better. Agreed?'

'Agreed,' I murmur. I've buried my head in soft puppy fur.

'And one more thing,' he says. 'Your mother might work with children and animals for a living, but she isn't actually that keen on them as a combination. So try to keep him and you out from under her feet, OK?'

I smile a bit at that.

He gets up and goes over the door.

He looks back at us on the bed when he gets there and he gives me a big wink.

'Dad,' I say, as he heads off downstairs. My voice is cracked with joy. 'Thanks.'

I spend the next three weeks walking Benjie, playing with Benjie and rushing home from school to stroke Benjie. He's adorable.

Mum mutters a bit about puppy puddles on the floor and fur all over her best white sofa, but she can see that Benjie is making me happy, so she grits her teeth and gives him a rather forced pat from time to time.

And I kind of feel less angry. I'm even OK at school, and things with Bindi are a bit better too, although I still get the feeling there's something she's not telling me.

Then one night a policeman comes to our front door just as we're eating supper.

I hear his low voice on the front door stop and then Dad shouts out, 'Oh no! Oh God, no!' and Mum leaps up from her chair in the kitchen and rushes to his side and her voice rises up into a panicking shriek, and I go dizzy and clutch onto the sides of my chair while the kitchen seems to whizz around in a circle.

Dad comes back into the kitchen with a grey face, and he's staggering like he's seen a ghost.

He sits down next to me.

He takes hold of my hand.

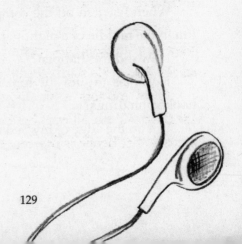

CHAPTER SEVENTEEN

The night after I find Jay slumped against his bed with the needle, I don't go to sleep at all.

I think I know what he was doing, but just to make sure, I log onto Dad's PC in the dead of night and google what I saw.

When I switch off the computer, I'm feeling like I'm in the middle of a nightmare.

How did this happen?

How has my lovely, fun big brother ended up hooked on drugs?

I sit on the edge of my bed all night and I think.

From time to time, bits of information pop up into my head, and I realise that Jay's been lost and lonely for quite a long time.

Some of the boys at school have started to laugh at him for having black hair and a white face and being obsessed with guitars.

He didn't tell me that, but I overheard a bunch of them talking outside school and using Jay's name, so I ducked behind a wall and crept closer so that I could eavesdrop.

'Reckons he's going to be a rock star,' said one boy.

'Yeah, he reckons he's really hard,' said another.

'Jay May, superstar,' said yet another. 'NOT. Have you seen his eyes? Wears more make-up than my mum.'

'He's such a loser,' said the first boy.

I think about all the times that Jay and I have been on our own at home while Dad's been on emergency call at the zoo and Mum's been out entertaining kids, and I realise that having a little sister to talk to hasn't been enough for Jay.

This thought hits me like a flying boot.

He's lonely, I think. No friends, no parents, only me.

And I wasn't enough to stop him doing drugs.

It's so awful realising this that I spend the entire night perched on the edge of my bed, chewing my nails and wondering what on earth to do next.

Jay warned me not to tell Mum and Dad

If I tell them, he'll never speak to me again.

But if I don't?

What will happen to him then?

In the end, I need to talk to somebody about it, so I wait until it's breakfast time the next day and I text Bindi and ask her to meet me early before school.

'If it's about that English essay forget it,' she says as we walk towards the school gates together. 'I didn't even understand the question.'

Then she takes a closer look at my pale face and places her slim brown hand on my arm.

Bindi's always been very kind and sensitive. She's not even thirteen at this point in our friendship, but her big eyes are full of concern, just like an adult.

'Spill,' she says, as we perch on a low wall outside the school.

I tell her about last night and what I found Jay doing and the things I read on the internet, and her eyes widen with shock. For a moment she just stares at me, like I'm some weird freak in a circus or something, except I know that's not why she's doing it, and I can see a hundred little brain wheels cranking into motion as Bindi tries to work out what on earth she can say that's going to help me.

In the end she says, 'It's kind of your decision, Lilah. I mean, he's not my brother, so it's not up to me to say what I would do.'

Oh.

I hoped she might be more helpful than that but I can see what she means.

'Maybe you could try and talk to Jay again first?' she says.

I've thought of that. Except that he scares me now.

My own brother scares me.

But I'm going to have to talk to him.

Soon.

* * *

It's hard to find the right time to talk to Jay.

He's hardly ever at home, and when he is, he's usually sleeping off the late nights he has nearly all the time now.

Mum's been down to his school to see the headmaster after they rang up and said that they hadn't seen Jay in lessons for over a week, and there's a huge scene at home with her screaming and him refusing to speak, and Dad banging on about how disappointed he is, and how the older child should set an example to the younger one. I hang my head and try not to catch Jay's eye. I hate being referred to as the little kid in all this, because after what I've seen in his bedroom I'm not feeling much like the innocent little sister any more.

I don't get to speak to him alone for almost a week, but then at last I get my chance because Mum and Dad decide that they need to go out to dinner alone and talk everything through, so they leave me in charge and head off to the local Indian.

I don't much want to be in charge.

I want things to be like they used to, with Jay looking after me and not the other way round. I'm only twelve, and I feel kind of sick and scared about all this.

And as if I'm totally on my own.

Jay stays up in his room for most of the evening, but in the end even he has to eat and drink sometimes, so he comes downstairs ravenous and I grill him some cheese-on-toast and he sits slumped at the kitchen table, sucking in the strings of yellow Cheddar in a way that makes me feel a bit sick.

I put a mug of tea in front of him and he empties the sugar bowl into it and gulps it down.

Gross.

I wait until he's finished, and then I take a deep slow breath.

'Jay,' I say. 'You know what you were doing the other night up in your room?'

Jay gives a brief nod. He's all wired up and shaky and can't sit still. Any moment now, he's going to bolt back upstairs. I have to be quick.

'Well, I think you should tell Mum and Dad,' I say. 'They might be able to help you.'

Jay gives an abrupt snort of laughter and gets up so fast that his chair falls over onto the kitchen floor.

'Get lost, Lilah,' he says. 'Like any of you bunch of losers can ever help me. They don't even notice whether I'm here or not most of the time.'

I swallow back a big lump of pain in my throat as my brother leaves the kitchen and goes upstairs to bang his bedroom door.

About an hour later I hear him throwing up in the bathroom, and then he comes downstairs walking in a wonky line, and slams out of the front door without even looking at me.

I sit at the table watching the clock for the rest of the evening, and have my second experience of the anger that's going to move into my life as a permanent guest.

It's like something rising up from my guts and making my breathing faster and my face tighten into a scowl.

By the time I hear my parents' key in the front door, I'm not the sweet little sister any longer.

I'm like a fired-up stick of rage-dynamite.

I've made my mind up.

I know what I have to do.

When I tell Mum and Dad about Jay and the drugs it feels like a relief for about, oh, thirty seconds.

'You did the right thing telling us, Lilah,' they say. Dad puts his arm around my shoulders and gives me a hug.

'Don't worry,' Mum says. Her voice is firm. 'We'll get it sorted out. The main thing is that we know what we're dealing with now.'

They pack me off to bed and I can hear the low hum of their voices in the kitchen as they discuss what they're going to say when Jay comes home.

I've got an awful sick feeling.

It doesn't feel right now, me telling Mum and Dad.

I wish I could rewind the whole afternoon and erase the words that came out of my mouth but it's a bit late for that.

I try really hard to stay awake, but I'm tired, so I drift off to sleep, and by the time I wake up it's the next morning and Jay's obviously been home because there are loads of messy plates and cups and things in the kitchen. I wait until Mum comes downstairs and starts tidying up, and I say, 'Did you talk to him about it?' and she says, 'Yes. It wasn't as bad as I thought, actually. He seemed a bit quiet, but he was taking in everything that Dad and I said to him.'

Dad's making toast and coffee to take up to Jay in bed.

'He's probably had to do a lot of thinking,' he says. 'He'll be wanting something to eat.'

I pour cereal into a white bowl and fill it up to the brim with milk. I've got tennis practice before school and I'm wearing my new white and green plimsolls, and I think that maybe things are actually going to get better now that it's all out in the open.

I'm just about to pack my bag and head off to school when Dad comes bolting down the stairs, taking them three at a time.

He runs to the front door and out into the drive, staring up and down our street, and then he comes back inside, sits down at the kitchen table and buries his head in his big, lion-taming hands.

'Jay's bed hasn't been slept in,' he says. 'He's gone.'

Jay doesn't come back at all that day.

Or the one after.

Or the one after that.

By then, my parents have already called the police and reported him missing.

I'm ashen with shock.

There's a huge space in the house where he ought to be.

My brother.

Gone.

And it's all because of me.

* * *

Four weeks after Jay goes missing, a television crew comes to our house.

They're making a programme about missing teenagers and they got in touch with us to see if we'd like their help.

Mum and Dad clutch at anything, so of course they say yes.

I don't say anything. Nobody asks me if I mind a television crew coming to the house. Nobody warns me that a teenage actor who looks a lot like Jay is going to take part in the reconstruction.

When I see him dressed up in Jay's clothes my heart feels faint, and I have to reach out and prop myself up against the hall wall until I get my breath back.

The boy traces Jay's last known movements, so he walks out of our house wearing black jeans and a black T-shirt and makes for the tube station, which is where Jay was last spotted by passers-by in the early hours of the morning he went missing. The passers-by are played by the actual people, and they're a middle-aged couple puffed up with importance at being on television, and concerned with getting their performance just right. I want to scream at them that this isn't some soap opera, it's our real family life that's happening, and we don't want to be on the television, we just want the missing part of our family back. But I don't say any of that, even though I'm wrecked with anger all the time.

The camera crew hang around our kitchen and Mum makes them cups of tea.

Her eyes have purple shadows underneath them from broken night after broken night, and she's stopped going to work and hired somebody else to take over her children's parties.

Dad's still going to the zoo, but he says his heart's not in it and he rings home several times a day to see how Mum is, and employs a new member of zoo staff to take over a lot of his duties.

I carry on going to school like a robot, but I can't take in a word of what's going on and only Bindi can get through to me.

A lot of the other kids whisper and point at me, but I'm beyond caring.

Our house has become so sad, like a hard shell full of bits of stuff that don't mean anything. The rooms feel cold and empty and just smell of furniture polish instead of spliffs and guitar-strings and trainers and junk food.

I watch the actor playing Jay as he does another take, walking out of our front door and down the street towards the tube station, and I wish harder than I've ever wished for anything in my life that it was really Jay and not some strange boy, and that I could run after him and grab him by the arm and say, 'Sorry, I'm sorry, Jay, I didn't mean to tell Mum and Dad and make you run away,' and persuade him to turn around and walk back into the house. But I know that's stupid, so I hang around the front garden with Dad, watching in silence and answering the odd question from the film crew. They carry on for the whole afternoon and I watch as the police talk to my parents while the filming drags on, and still I can only think of the one question that's been haunting me day and night ever since he went.

When will Jay come home again?

CHAPTER EIGHTEEN

Two years and two months after the day he went missing, the police reckon that they might have found Jay.

Dad's holding my hand in the kitchen.

He talks in a very soft and steady voice, not like his usual loud bark. It's the voice he uses when he has to climb into an enclosure of lions and break up a fight, or rescue a trapped cub, or give an injection.

Except that he doesn't need to tame me on this particular day.

142

I've lost the power of speech and I'm the quietest I've ever been.

Even Benjie's gone quiet and is huddled under my chair.

Behind the dark bulk of Dad's head I can see Mum leaning on the banisters in the hall and hiding her face behind her hand. There's a policewoman standing next to her with one hand on Mum's elbow and she's bent towards Mum in concern. I make out the words 'tea' and 'sit down' and 'when you're ready,' but I can't make any sense of it, because I feel as if a big part of my side has been ripped off and left all the inside bits of me hanging out.

Jay.

Jay.

I want Jay.

Dad's stroking my hair, and he has big tears rolling down his face. I've almost never seen Dad cry. Even when Jay went missing the first time, he didn't cry. He just went grey and aged about twenty years in five minutes and ever since then he's not smiled or laughed in the way that he used to.

Mum's been the one who cries.

She's crying again now, like her heart is broken.

The policewoman comes into the kitchen and fills

up the kettle, hunts for cups and mugs and gets milk out of the fridge.

'We will need you to come and make an identification,' she says to Dad, with an anxious look at me. 'Your daughter should probably stay at home.'

'It's OK, I'm nearly sixteen,' I say, out of habit. People always think I look younger than I am. They should see Bindi – she still looks about twelve.

At the thought of my best friend, I find a rush of tears coming up from somewhere and I reach in my pocket for my phone.

'Can I call Bindi?' I say.

Dad nods.

'You're not to come with us, Lilah,' he says. 'This is for me and Mum to do on our own.'

I'm too dazed to argue, so I just give him a nod back and then I go into the hallway and dial Bindi's mobile, but it's switched off, so I have to dial her landline instead.

'Hello, love,' says Reeta. 'She's just upstairs. Are you OK, Lilah? You sound very serious.'

I manage to squawk out a 'Yes, I'm fine,' and then there's a pause, during which I can hear the blast of Asian Network getting nearer and nearer as Reeta moves upstairs with the phone, and then it's turned down and Bindi's soft voice comes onto the line. She already seems alarmed, because her mum's obviously told her that I sound weird, and Bindi knows me really well so I don't have to say all that much.

I just say, 'They think they've found Jay. But it's not good news. Can you come?' and she throws the phone down and is already on her way by the time I go back downstairs again, to where the policewoman is leading Mum and Dad towards the front door.

Mum comes back just as they are about to go.

She gives me the fiercest hug she's ever given me. It squeezes every bone and rib and muscle in my body and snatches my breath away.

'We'll ring you,' she says. 'Stay here with Bindi. Stay *safe*, Lilah.' And they walk down the path behind the policewoman and get into the car in complete silence.

I watch them sitting stiff and upright in the back of the police car, not speaking, and then I listen to the sound of the car pulling away in the rain. The streets are all wet and shiny and there's a smell of damp grass in the air.

No stars out tonight, and no moon.

Just the clouds, moving in silence across the streetlights.

I turn and walk back inside the house. It already looks and smells different.

With no Jay and now no Mum and Dad, it's a building sucked clean of family and warmth. A shell.

I sit on the stairs in the hall in the dark and Benjie comes and huddles next to me. I bury my head in his warm fur and wrap my arms over both of us to make a warm, dark burrow of dog and girl.

Five minutes later, Bindi rings the bell.

∗ ∗ ∗

It feels like the longest night ever.

Mum rings me to say they've arrived and that they're going to be quite a while.

I don't ask any questions. That's because I don't want to know the answers.

Instead, I let Bindi make me a mug of hot chocolate with loads of milk and sugar and we take y room and sit on the bed for a while with . and she makes me tip all my jewellery out on the duvet and tries to make me laugh by putting it on and making silly comments. I sort of go along with it and even laugh a real laugh at one point, and then I'm tripped up with guilt for laughing when I know what Mum and Dad are going to have to do. I find that I'm shaking like I've got the flu, so Bindi just creeps over to my side of the bed and hugs me until I stop, which is about ten minutes later, when I'm exhausted and feel all cold and thin.

'Don't be nice to me,' I growl, in a more Lilah-like way. 'It might make me cry.'

Fat chance of that, but she knows what I mean.

Bindi switches Planet Rock on and finds some good heavy metal music, and demands that I show her how to head-bang so I do. For a moment it feels good to thrash about to the hard beat of the music, and a little part of me thinks that Jay might actually be watching me from somewhere and grinning at me, like he used to do before it all went wrong.

'Yeah, Liles – you look so cool doing that, NOT,' I hear in my head.

There's a faint whiff of Jay in the bedroom for a moment. Sweat, spliffs, guitars and hair gel. Then it floats away as quickly as it came.

I start to shake again.

Bindi holds my hand.

I don't know what makes me want to do this, but I take Bindi into Jay's room later on.

The last time she came into his room was when he still lived at home, before he started going all weird. He used to be really nice to my mates and chat to them about school and music and silly stuff.

Now Bindi's creeping about like a non-believer in a church, trying not to touch anything until I give her an exasperated shove.

'He's not exactly going to mind if you mess anything up, is he?' I say, with a hint of my anger coming back.

Bindi is kind enough not to snap back at me. She picks up a pile of tatty old copies of NME magazine and leafs through them with a bemused look on her delicate face.

'I've never heard of any of these bands,' she says. 'Why haven't I?'

I grin.

''Cos you only listen to Asian music,' I say. 'Jay was really into his indie stuff. His band played loads of it. You know, like the stuff Adam Carter plays now.'

Bindi gives a slight jump when I say this. Or at least, I think she does. My mind's all over the place. I might have imagined it.

She's staring at me now with a look I can't quite work out.

'What?' I say. 'What are you thinking?'

'If I say it,' she says, 'you'll think I'm really mad. Or selfish.'

I smile.

'You, selfish?' I say. 'Go on – just say it.'

'Well,' says Bindi. 'I know this is a terrible time for your family. And I know you really miss Jay. But, the thing is – I'm kind of a bit jealous of you sometimes.'

I'm so surprised at this, that I nearly slide off the side of Jay's bed.

'Me?' I say. 'My life is totally rubbish. Why would you be jealous of me?'

Bindi sighs and looks around Jay's bedroom.

'This,' she says. 'Your own bedrooms. One each. I have to share with two of my sisters.'

I glance around at Jay's posters. I've never really thought about it.

'And,' Bindi continues. I can feel her gathering pace. 'And your mum and dad give you loads and loads of attention. There's always one of them there for you to talk to.'

I give this a bit of thought.

'It feels like they were never there for us,' I say. 'It's part of why Jay went missing, I reckon. They were caught up in their jobs all the time.'

Bindi is shaking her head.

'No,' she says. 'I can tell you what it's like to have parents who never listen to you, never even notice if you are home sometimes. And all the attention is focused on the little kids, not on me. Believe me, Lilah – you're lucky.'

I don't feel very lucky, what with my parents having gone off to identify a body that may or may not be my brother, but she looks so sad that I don't have the heart to make that dig, so I don't.

I play Bindi some Manic Street Preachers instead, even though it kills my heart to hear the familiar songs, and she puts on this sort of fixed smile and taps her foot along, which looks really weird. I can tell she hates it, so I take it off again.

I dig out some of the photographs of Jay's first gig and we look at them in silence.

There's Ben, his lead singer, all spiky black hair and screwed-up face, howling some song into the microphone.

There's Eddie, their drummer, head down, blonde shaggy hair over his face and the sweat shining on his bare chest.

There's Matt, the keyboard player, standing with his legs apart in a typical rock-star pose, his long fair hair limp and parted in the centre. He's the one who sent me the Facebook message.

And there's Jay. My brother. Lead guitar. Not posing, or grimacing. He's wearing a black T-shirt and black jeans and his dark hair wasn't so straight then, so there's a wing of curls dipping over one eye. He's looking down at his fingers on the fretboard of his guitar as if he's really concentrating on the music, and he's holding the neck of the guitar with care, like you'd hold an egg in your hand.

It was all about the music for Jay.

That guitar sits alone in the corner of his bedroom now.

I pick it up and run my hands over the strings, stroke the smooth polished surface and feel my way past the little switches and knobs on the front.

'Can I?' says Bindi.

I shrug.

'Why not?' I say. 'He wouldn't mind.'

I pass the heavy instrument over to Bindi

and she strikes what she thinks is a Rock God pose with it. She looks so ridiculous in her pink jewelled clothes and nose-stud, holding a red Les Paul guitar, that I find myself laughing until my stomach hurts. Then she starts to laugh as well, and we're both laughing so loud that for a moment we don't hear the phone with its shrill, insistent tone cutting into the dark hallway outside, but then Benjie starts to bark and our smiles fade, and we leave the guitar on the bed and bolt downstairs.

I snatch up the receiver and can't speak for a moment, I'm so out of breath.

Bindi hovers behind me with one light hand on my shoulder.

'Lilah?' says Dad's voice. He sounds heavy, broken. I can hear Mum crying in the background.

'It's not him,' he says. 'Lilah. It's OK. It's not Jay.'

I drop the phone and fall to my knees.

Bindi speaks to my dad and then hangs up.

She puts her arms around me.

We sit in the dark hall on the carpet.

I'm shaking so hard that I head-butt her in the teeth at one point.

'It doesn't matter,' she says, when I apologise.

She's right.

Nothing else matters.

LILAH'S ANGER DIARY APRIL 28th (Bedtime)
ANGER LEVELS: 4/10

I'm so relieved. We've been lucky. It's not Jay who's been found dead. This time.

CHAPTER NINETEEN

<u>LILAH'S ANGER DIARY</u>   MAY 3rd

ANGER LEVELS: »8/10«

Not sure how much more I can handle. I was getting better because of Benjie, but I'm still angry with Jay for putting us through all this. I miss him. I miss him more than ever. I just want to know that he's OK.

And despite what Bindi says, I'm angry with Mum and Dad for never being there when Jay needed them. Or when I needed them. I'm angry that Jay's mates deserted him and he felt the need to try drugs and then run away from home. Most of all, I'm angry with one person for what she did and the mess she made of all this.

And that one person is me.

* * *

In the few days after we find out that it wasn't Jay who was found in the river, we tiptoe around the house in a kind of numb shock.

None of us can say his name, but from time to time we give each other a wan smile of relief mixed up with anguish, because we're still no nearer to finding him. We still don't know whether he's dead or alive.

Adam rings up to see how I am, but I can hardly speak.

'*Groo*,' I manage.

It seems a good time to use a Lilah-ism. I can't find any normal words that even get close to painting how I feel inside.

'OK,' says Adam. 'Well, I'm glad it wasn't Jay. That means you can kind of have hope again, yeah?'

I can't answer. My head is so muddled up that I don't know what I want any more.

Dad takes a day off work, which is dead unusual.

'Somebody else can look after the lions,' he says. 'We need some family time.'

He's probably right. But the thought of having

155

to spend an entire day with the Old Dudes is stressing me out a bit.

'You can take a day off school, Lilah,' says Mum. 'Just this once.'

My heart sinks into my biker boots.

The one good thing about school is that it keeps me getting up in the mornings. That, Planet Rock and Bindi, with her shy smile and her gentle voice. She's texted me about a million times since she spent the evening here.

Reeta dropped by with a huge dish of homemade Indian food the next night.

When Mum opened the door and took the hot dish full of fragrant, spicy smells, both women burst into tears and there was lots of hugging.

'Thank God,' whispered Reeta. 'Thank God it wasn't your boy, Rachel.'

So I reckon that I'm going to have to do Family Day, seeing as I'm part of this family and we haven't exactly been having the best time lately.

'Where shall we go?' asks Dad. 'Park? It's a nice day out there.'

So we end up in the park, just the three of us, strolling along past the lake and the Chinese Pagoda and the wooden hut where they serve teas, and to anybody sitting on a bench and watching us pass by, we probably look just like a normal family having a lovely day out together.

Except that the May family is anything but normal.

Dad buys us ice creams from the hut and we do a lap of the park, going towards the swings where I messed about with Adam Carter. Even though that was only a few weeks ago, it feels like about a hundred years.

We don't talk much. I make a great play out of swiping the top of the ice cream off with my tongue.

I see Mum cast a look towards the swings out of the corner of her eye, and then she catches Dad's, and he puts his arm around her shoulders.

I stare at the empty orange plastic seats tipping slightly in the breeze, and I see myself aged about six sitting on one of them and gripping the greasy chains tight in my hot hands. Jay's behind me, with his big mop of hair lifting in the breeze. He's wearing a striped blue and white T-shirt and brown shorts and he's pushing me up into the air with a shout of effort, and I'm screaming with happiness and feeling the hot sun on my cheeks and the *whoosh* of the air as I sink down and fly up again, and my stomach's doing that sinking thing like I'm on a roller coaster. Somewhere in the background Mum and Dad are two little dots sitting on a bench with bags of sandwiches and a rolled-up rug ready for a picnic.

I watch my parents now trying not to look at the swings, and that flicker of anger starts to burn up my insides again. Except this time it doesn't stop, but boils up into this great big, tense, tight feeling. I just know it's going to all burst out of my mouth and I can't stop it, so I open my mouth and let it out, and even I am frightened by the yelling, but my gob's taken on a mind of its own and I can't do anything about it.

'I'm SICK of hiding my feelings because of Jay!' I yell.

Mum and Dad both jump at the tone of my voice and the unexpected explosion.

Dad takes a step towards me, but no amount of taming is going to stop this one.

'I'm sick of not being able to talk about Jay without you getting in a state or having a go at me or getting all upset!' I scream.

A flock of pigeons that were pecking at a half-eaten sandwich on the tarmac rise up in a big panicky flight of flapping wings.

'And I'm angry that Jay felt lonely all the time!'

I continue. 'And I'm fed up not being myself in case I upset anybody. OK? OK?'

I take my denim jacket off and chuck it on the grass. Then I head off to the swing and sit down on the orange plastic seat. The sharp plastic sides cut into my bottom.

Mum puts one hand over her mouth and stops dead in her tracks.

'It's OK,' says Dad. 'It's probably a good idea. She needs to let her feelings out.'

He comes over to where I'm sitting and stands behind me. I feel his big, lion-taming hands on my waist and then there's a gentle push. I just about get my feet off the ground, and then come skittering down again with my feet trailing in the gravel underneath.

'Pathetic,' I say. 'I'm fifteen, not six. You'll have to push a bit harder than that.'

'Aren't you breaking the park rules?' says Mum. 'You're a bit old for swings now, aren't you Lilah?'

Dad and I give her a scathing look of impatience.

'Purleease,' I say. 'What are you, some sort of *ruletarian*?'

She laughs and wipes her eyes with a handkerchief.

'Oh Lilah,' she says. 'Fair enough.'

Then Mum looks around the park like a naughty child caught bunking off school. She sits down on the swing next to me and grabs the chains and closes her eyes tight while Dad gives her an enormous push into the air, and before we know it, he's darting between us both and we're flying up into the air with our legs sticking out in front of us, Mum in her sensible knee-length blue skirt and flat shoes, and me all black-jeaned and booted. We scream out like we're kids, and for just a moment while I'm up there, I close my eyes in the warmth of the sun and imagine it's Jay below on the ground, staring up at me and waiting for me to come back down so that he can give me another push, and the feeling is so sweet that I smile a pure smile of happiness.

But then it's sucked away again almost as soon as it comes, and the chill of what's real hits me in the stomach like a bag of rusty nails. I come down, snatch my black denim jacket up from the grass, dig my hands deep into the pockets and head off across the park without a word. Mum and Dad have the sense to just let me go, and when I get to the park gates and glance back, they're standing together by the swings, two tiny, dark stick-figures, and I can tell that Mum is crying again from the way that Dad is bending over her.

I still haven't cried since the day Jay left, over two years ago.

The tears just won't come.

CHAPTER TWENTY

<u>LILAH'S ANGER DIARY</u> AUGUST 5th

ANGER LEVELS: 5/10

Things are getting a bit better. I said sorry for the way I exploded in the park that day, and the Old Dudes were really nice about it. They actually bothered to listen to me say how I am feeling, and they said that they understood and weren't angry. Shockerola!

It's summer hols now, and I get to lie in bed late and not do any homework – awesome! Now all we need is for Jay to come home.

***

Somehow, I don't really know how, we manage to get through the next three months and fix up some sort of family life again.

It's like the shell of our old family life, but at least it feels kind of safe and full of routine, and it's the nearest we ever get to being normal again, so I'm glad.

Mum finally goes back to work full-time, but they have a big talk with me first about how I'm feeling, and she agrees not to do any more Sunday parties. Dad decides to cut down his hours at Morley Zoo so that he can be at home a lot more while I'm on summer holidays, and although I'm still angry a lot of the time, I make a super-human effort to try and be nice, because I can see that they're doing all this for me. And I love Benjie to pieces and it's not fair on him if I'm snappy all the time, so we go on loads of walks and runs in the park, and it all helps me feel less angry.

One evening Bindi rings me up in tears and asks if I can come over.

'Spill,' I say, sitting cross-legged on her bed, where I'm trying on all her rings and bracelets.

'You're scaring me. You never cry.'

It's true. Bindi hardly ever gets upset about anything. I know it must be something quite rubbish, as I haven't seen her cry since her cat died three years ago.

She takes a big shuddering breath through her tears and looks down past her elegant narrow nose while she gathers up strength to speak.

It takes another minute, during which I become aware of some gorgeous cooking smells wafting upstairs, and my stomach starts leaping about with hunger because I left home without having any supper.

'Bind,' I say. 'It's me, Lilah. You can tell me anything. I mean, how bad can it be? It's not like you're going to tell me you're pregnant or anything, is it?'

I fall back on her pink quilt laughing at my own witty joke, and then I become aware of something odd.

Bindi's not laughing.

I sit bolt upright in fright.

'You're not!' I say. 'No. You can't be. You don't *do* boys.'

The next silence is really heavy. I didn't know

164

that a silence could be so loaded full of stuff, like it's about to vomit it all out over the quilt, and flood the room and the hallway outside.

'Omigod,' I say. 'This is, like, total *stresserola*.' Trust me to slip in a Lilah-ism at that point. I always do it when I'm nervous, and Bindi's making me seriously nervous now.

'Who?' I say. 'Who did you sleep with?'

There's another silence.

Somehow the silences are doing all the answering for Bindi. She doesn't need to actually say a word.

I feel my legs start to tremble and go sweaty, so I stand up by the bed and look down at the shiny black hair on the crown of her head and the neat parting in the middle of her scalp. As I do that, it's as if everything that there's ever been between us just sort of slides away into a big bin of no return, and the whole framework of my rubbish teenage life crumbles and shakes with an earthquake that might actually register on some scale somewhere, and then it collapses to the ground around my feet.

'Lilah, wait,' whispers Bindi, as I head for the door. 'It was all a horrid mistake. He just showed some interest in me and I'd been feeling really miserable at home, that's all. I'm sorry.'

'But you don't DO boys!' I yell. 'You're going to have an arranged marriage!'

Bindi dissolves into more tears.

'But that doesn't mean I'm happy with the idea, does it?' she whispers.

For a nano-second I look at my best mate in floods of tears and my heart leaps with pity for her, but then a vision of her and Adam pushes that aside and I realise that if I don't want to lash out at Bindi, then I'd better leave.

I shut the bedroom door behind me with admirable quietness.

Then I walk home kicking at every wall and every wheel of every car until my foot is throbbing, my eyes are screwed up in pain, my teeth are glued together and I've used as many rude words as I can find. Then I go home, slam upstairs, bang my bedroom door, and I sit on the bed and bang the back of my head on the cream-coloured wallpaper again and again until my brain feels dull and fuzzy.

She lied to me! BINDI. She's been lying to me for ages and ages.

The one person I thought I could rely on.

I close my eyes and continue to thud my brain to pulp on the wall behind me.

After a while my head goes numb, and little fragments of film start running through my mind.

I remember Bindi's sad face up in her bedroom while her little brother and sisters ran about the house yelling. And how she was quiet and withdrawn at school some days and hid herself away in the library to study.

With a pang, I realise that Bindi's been really, really lonely.

And that maybe sleeping with Adam meant that she had somebody who liked her, and wanted to spend time with her.

And that maybe I could have spent a bit more time with her myself, if I hadn't been so caught up in Jay all the time.

I bang my head against the wall again, but this time I'm angry with myself as well as with Bindi.

Usually, when I have a mood, my parents ignore me because they're too busy stressing out about Jay, but tonight I'm in for a surprise.

Dad bounds upstairs to my bedroom and comes in without knocking.

It isn't actually a Taming Lilah day, but he watches me banging my head for a moment longer, and then he comes over and sits on the bed next to me and places his hands on my shoulders.

Dad pulls me away from the wall.

His hands feel very strong and firm on the tops of my arms.

'Geroff,' I mutter, trying not to look at him. 'You don't care. You care more about animals than you do about me. Or Jay. He felt lonely. You and Mum were never here for him when it mattered.'

He tips my chin up so that I have to look him in the eye, and then he speaks to me in the voice he keeps for untamed lions and angry tigers, and I know from the way his eyes are full of hurt and sadness that I've gone too far this time, and that he doesn't really love his animals more than me or Jay.

'Enough, Lilah,' is all he says, but it works. It's what I need to hear.

'Enough.'

✳ ✳ ✳

I drift through life for a few days. It's difficult going into town. Sometimes I run into Bindi, and even though I cross the street and walk away, I can feel her anguished eyes boring into the back of my head and carving out the word 'SORRY' in my skull. I know full well that she really IS sorry, and that she has her own problems and I should have noticed them like a proper best mate would have done.

One day she catches me out.

My mobile rings while I'm out shopping with Mum, so I answer it without looking to see who's calling me.

'Lilah, it's me,' she says. 'Don't hang up!'

I catch my breath and put my finger over the red button which will cut her off, but somehow I can't quite press it. I want to hear what she's got to say, even though another part of me doesn't want to hear anything at all from her ever again.

'What do you want?' I say.

Mum is making faces at me. Big, encouraging smiles and dramatic nodding of her head. She knows all about what's happened with Bindi.

'To say sorry,' whispers Bindi. 'I really am. And now I'm in such a mess, Lilah. I don't know what to do.'

I walk out of the shop and leave Mum holding up a black cardigan and screwing up her mouth in concentration in front of the mirror.

There's a wall outside in the car park and I sit on it and swivel my legs up into the sun, hugging my knees.

'Spill,' I say. Bindi gives a small laugh.

'Stop using my expressions, Lilah May,' she says, and for a moment it's like the sun just got a bit brighter.

'Adam's going to stick by me,' she says, and it feels like the sun's gone straight back in again, to be replaced by a thundering black sky.

My heart misses a beat and then makes a deep twang.

Heartache, I think. *This is really what it feels like*.

'Yeah?' I say. 'That's big of him.'

I curse myself for being snappy and angry yet again, but it's too late to pull back what I've just said, so I don't even try.

Bindi's trying not to cry.

'My mum and dad are going to support me and we're going to bring up the baby together at home,' she says.

I laugh. It's not exactly what Bindi's mother had planned for her daughter.

'It's not funny, actually,' says Bindi. Her voice has taken on an edge that I've never heard before. 'When I first told Mum, she screamed at me and shut herself in the bedroom and cried for hours. Dad wasn't exactly over the moon either. He said that I had let the entire family down.'

I've never seen Bindi's mother, Reeta, look anything other than calm and smiley.

'So no more arranged marriages,' I say. 'You must be pleased about that.'

Bindi sniffles and gives a small hiccup.

'Pleased?' she says. 'How can I be pleased? My parents say that they've wasted money on my education. I've upset everybody and ruined my life. And now I've ruined our friendship too, haven't I?'

I know that at this point I am supposed to be calm and reassuring and say that of course I'll stick with her to the ends of time, no matter what.

But then Adam's lovely face and punk hair shoot in front of my eyes and I get that pang again. Adam Carter. He was supposed to be mine.

'I don't know,' I say. 'I need some time to think about all this. Sorry.'

Then I press the red button on my phone and go back to join Mum.

* * *

The next few days are kind of odd.

There's a really weird feeling in the air at the moment.

I feel like I'm on the brink of something and I don't know what.

Something has shifted in the air inside the house, too.

The atmosphere feels less heavy and flat, and more charged up with something.

'Are you premenstrual, love?' says Mum, when I try to explain.

Helpful. Not.

Dad comes home all excited after a rare white tiger gives birth at the zoo.

He takes me to see the cubs and lets me inside their pen to stroke their soft white fur.

The cubs have giant floppy paws that seem nearly as big as their heads, and they lurch from side to side and flop over into furry balls from time to time.

For about an hour I forget about everything at home and school, and I'm just transfixed by the cubs as they roll about and play with each other. I watch my dad handle them and I feel kind of proud, but I can't tell him, of course, because that's soppy and embarrassing. I used to be really fed up that

Dad loved animals more than me, and I'm better at anger than lovely sentiments, so I don't say anything, but it's a really good Father-Daughter day, and we drive home in a calm sort of mood, with Dad whistling and me sucking on a bag of strawberry liquorice strings and idly wondering if I should go shopping at the weekend and buy the black leather buckle boots I've been craving for weeks.

And when we get home, Mum's made a huge lasagne from scratch and she lets me have a small glass of red wine with it, and for once, the three of us manage to stay in the same room for a whole evening and have something almost like a normal conversation, with some laughter too. And because of the laughter, I don't hear the buzz of my mobile phone at first, not until it gets louder and starts to leap around in my pocket.

I excuse myself and go off into another room, because I'm pretty sure it's Bindi again and she'll want to speak to me in private, and all I can do is ask her to give me more time to think about our friendship. So I whip out the phone and answer it in a silly voice so that she'll feel encouraged to speak to me, and there's a long silence and a few crackles on the other end, so I say, 'Hello? Bind?' again.

And then it comes.

It comes at me out of the past.

Out of the dark.

Out of a time I thought I'd lost.

Out of two years of grief. Anger. Hopelessness.

'Liles?' says the voice. 'Is that you?'

CHAPTER
TWENTY-ONE

I fall.

My legs just give way underneath me, and I'm sprawled on the floor with my hands shaking so hard that I drop the phone and have to pick it up again.

'Yes,' I say in the tiniest whisper. 'It's me.'

Oh.

Oh.

Please let this not be a cruel trick.

'Where are you?' I say. 'Are you OK?'

There's another short silence.

'I'm OK,' he says. 'I'm not coming home. I just wanted to tell you that I'm OK.'

His voice sounds thin and tired. Older.

My tears are starting to come. At last.

I wipe my nose and grip the handset so hard that it hurts.

'Jay,' I say. 'Oh Jay. Do you forgive me?'

There's a series of beeping noises on the line and then a click and a dead sort of humming noise.

He's gone.

'No,' I whisper. 'No, no, no, you can't go yet, don't go, don't go.'

I press the call button on my mobile but it says *Number Withheld*.

I make it into the downstairs loo just in time.

I vomit for what seems like an age, and when I lift my head, all damp with sweat and tears, Mum and Dad are standing there with faces like ghosts. I lurch up and stagger into their arms, and I cry out two year's worth of pent-up tears, and all my anger leaves my body like a flood.

I'd forgotten what tears felt like. Great big fat ones roll down my face and drip off my chin onto the floor like some sort of tear production line in a factory, while I hiccup and gasp for breath, and feel my nostrils getting blocked and my eyes puffing into little swollen slits, but I can't stop crying.

My anger just melts away. I swear I feel it flood out of my body, slink along the floor in a watery line and squeeze itself under the door before making its way down the hall and out of the front door.

It's nearly an hour before I can speak properly, so I just whisper his name over and over and wave my mobile around in front of me, and they go pale and sink to their knees. The three of us hug and cry right by the rim of the toilet and we don't even care.

Jay.

My big brother.

It's OK.

I heard his voice.

He's alive.

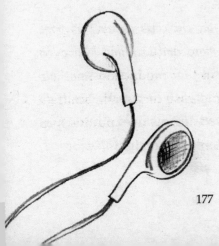

177

CHAPTER TWENTY-TWO

LILAH'S ANGER DIARY AUGUST 6th
ANGER LEVELS: 2/10
Lowest ever !!

I've got hope now. Jay might come home.

Mum and Dad are being really cool at last. Not that I'm going to tell them that! We have a Family Day every Saturday, and the three of us go out somewhere and try not to kill each other.

Mum's now doing a tai chi class as well as yoga to reduce her stress levels more, and Dad and I have 'an understanding'. We don't have Taming Lilah sessions any more, but if I start kicking off, he just puts his hands on my shoulders again and uses the calm voice he uses on Lazarus, and he tells me it's enough. And it kind of works, 'cos I'm not so angry any more.

* * *

I'm dreaming.

It's an Indian summer September, many years ago.

We're on a beach and the sand is so hot, it burns the soles of our feet and clings to our wet legs when we run away from the frothy waves, screaming with delight.

I've spent the whole afternoon crouched over a rock-pool. There are rough-shelled limpets clinging to the rocks and little orange spider crabs scuttling sideways, trying to get away from my childish fingers and tiny green fishing-net.

I've got a jar full of water-snails clutched in my hands, and I'm treading on the wiggly worm casts in the damp brown sand that always reminds me of Dad's special sugar for putting on porridge.

Dad's lying half-buried, pretending to groan in agony as Jay piles on more sand with a red plastic spade.

Mum's eating a choc-ice with a faraway look in her eyes, but whenever she sees me, she grabs me and rubs sticky coconut gunk into my skin to protect me from the sun, and all the sand gets rubbed in with it so that I make a face and a squeal of protest.

'Look,' I say, displaying my bounty of snails.

'Horrible, Lilah,' says Mum, but she's smiling. 'Why don't you both go for one more dip in the sea? We've got to pack up soon.'

She glances up at the sky. The sun's still hot, but in an hour it will begin to get chilly on the beach. Most people are already packing up their windbreaks and picnics and heading towards the small ramp that leads up from the white beach to the car park beyond.

'Jay?' I say, in my high, six-year-old voice. 'Please will you paddle with me?'

I'm not allowed to go in on my own. It's big sea here, with real white horses on the tips of the waves, and they just might ride off with a small girl.

My brother groans and rolls his eyes, but he stabs his red spade into the damp sand and ignores Dad's cries of protest at being left half-buried.

We skip down to the edge of the water, just like we've done a thousand times before, and yet this time feels kind of different, more special. And my own voice in the dream, older, says, 'You'll remember this,' and so I grip Jay's hand a bit tighter and look up at my nine-year-old brother as we race over the froth and plunge into the waters.

His curly brown hair catches the light and I can see freckles forming over the bridge of his nose.

'Jay?' I say. He's kicking at the waves now, splashing me on purpose.

I squeal and jump about in my blue swimsuit with the little white skirt.

'We'll always be together, won't we?' I say, shielding my eyes against the sun.

'Yeah, course we will, Liles,' comes a voice, but it doesn't sound like Jay.

I squint against the brightness of the sun.

There's his shadow looming over me.

We're so close that I can smell his suntan lotion.

I try really hard, but it's impossible.

I just can't see his face.

'Lilah, Jay,' calls Mum. 'We're going now.'

I give her the thumbs up, and then I turn back to my brother.

I wait.

I reckon the clouds will pass.

If you enjoyed

you can visit www.taminglilahmay.co.uk
for more news and information.

Read on for an exclusive preview
of the follow-up,

CHAPTER ONE

'You should ring Bindi, love,' Mum says. 'It's the right thing to do. You two were such good friends!'

I sigh. It's nearly the half-term holiday and I don't know what's right or wrong any more

I'm not even sure who I am.

It's been a rubbish start to autumn. Mum and Dad are a bit stressed at the moment and, although I know why, it's starting to make me angry. I have a slight problem with anger, you see. It doesn't take much for me to flare up into a rage or to start snapping at Mum or sulking with Dad.

My parents are not, and never have been, exactly 'normal'.

My mother is a clown. Yes, really. She entertains kids at children's parties and she used to be good at it until our family kind of fell to pieces. Then recently she decided to spend more time with me and go to extra yoga classes to keep herself calm, but over the last few weeks I can see that she's getting restless and really wants to go back full-time to her job as a clown. My dad tames lions and he's quite good at 'taming' *me* when I get angry but he spends most of his waking hours obsessing about big cats. Sometimes I wish I had a furry mane and a big set of teeth and claws because then he might pay me more attention.

We kind of got a bit hopeful because my brother – Jay – rang up after two years of us not knowing whether he was alive or dead.

I asked him if he forgave me for what I did and the line made this loud humming noise and he wasn't there any more.

We couldn't call him back but the police have been trying to trace the phone box he called from.

Jay still hasn't come home.

And Bindi?

She let me down.

Big time.

Imagine the worst thing that a best friend could do to you, and then triple it. Well, that's what Bindi did to me.

Groo.

***

Vanessa Curtis
spent the best part of a decade playing
in very loud rock bands which is why
she can't remember much about her twenties.
However, these days her brother plays in a band,
so she can leave the wild partying to him and
concentrate on writing books for children instead.
She lives near Chichester Harbour with her
husband and cat and still likes to crank up Planet
Rock to full volume when there's nobody in.
Vanessa is the award-winning author
of *Zelah Green* and *Zelah Green:*
One More Little Problem.

Vist Vanessa's website at
www.vanessacurtis.com

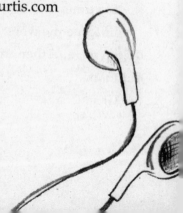